DEATH

&

DEPRAVITY

by

ARTHUR COLE

&

NIGEL WILLIAMS

February 2016.

First Edition.

ISBN – 13:978-1530437429

ISBN – 10:1530437423

Artcymru Publications.

Arthur Cole joined the Glamorgan Police at the age of seventeen. At nineteen, he joined the South Wales Constabulary as a constable and was stationed at Bridgend.

After nearly four years working beats, he became a detective constable, covering the whole division.

During his service, he dealt with every kind of major crime committed in the area, including murder and rape before joining Special Branch where he worked until he retired after thirty years of service.

In 1975, he met Caroline, his wife, who was also a serving police officer at the time. Caroline left the force in 1980 to raise their family whilst Arthur continued within the service and later became a Detective Sergeant. They have two children.

Upon retirement, Arthur became a gardener and enjoys golf and all sports as well as writing poetry. **"Unethical Conduct"** is his first novel, written in collaboration with Nigel Williams who is also a former police officer and now a lecturer in Fine Art at a college in Swansea.

Nigel joined the Metropolitan Police in 1981 and was posted to Brixton. In 1984, he transferred home to South Wales where he worked beats and became a Traffic officer. He was also authorised for the use of firearms and became a VIP and Special Escort Group driver.

In 1994, Nigel was hit by a stolen car on duty and fractured his spine. During recovery, he retrained and achieved a first-class (honours) degree in fine art. He then gained a teaching qualification from Cardiff University and a master's degree from Swansea.

Nigel has been married to Caroline for twenty-seven years and has three children and a granddaughter and a dog called Zac.

This is Nigel's second collaboration. The first being **No Step Back** by Alan Lloyd MBE.

Other books by Nigel Williams also writing as N Williams and NC Williams:

Eden Relics (2012)

Welsh Gold (2012)

Fake Baked (2012)

No Step Back With Alan Lloyd MBE (2015)

A Hard Place (2015)

A Cold Place (2016)

Coming July 2016:

A Dead Place

Terry McGuire Series of Thrillers

Unethical Conduct (2016)

Edge of Integrity

Death and Depravity

Angel of Death

Coming May 2016

Nest of Vipers

Sign up for updates of new book releases and a free download of Fake Baked by N.C. Williams by sending your email address directly to: nigel699@sky.com

First published in Great Britain by Artcymru Publishing (AC Books) 2016.

THE STRIKE

February 27th 1985.

It hadn't been quite what he'd expected. He truly believed it had been the right thing to do, but the strike had cost him his home and pushed his family to breaking point. Nobody believed it was going to last so long. At the outset, the word from the Union was that the Government would fold in double-quick time, that Thatcher's talk of breaking the union was just a load of party-political bluster. The National Union of Mineworkers had won a battle against the government before and they could win again, as long as everybody stayed out. But everybody hadn't stayed out. The scabs had undermined the strike and caused a serious friction with the police that had left wounds Michael believed would never be healed. Brother had turned against brother, father against son. The whole thing had become a bloody mess.

St. David's Day was just around the corner and things had never looked so bleak. The news from the union was bad. Everyone expected the strike to end in the next day or so. If it did, it would signal the end for the coalmines in Wales and probably the rest of the U.K. too.

Michael Jeffrey Foley had moved the family into a one-bedroom house owned by a family friend. He had been lucky to get it after losing their own to the mortgage company. There were so many of the strikers in the same position, all desperately looking for alternative accommodation after their savings had run dry and the bailiffs had moved in to take away everything they had spent their lives working for. At least his friend had given him six-months - rent free - to help get him through the bad times, but then he'd have to either find a new job, if the garage work didn't improve, or somehow get onto the Council house rental stock waiting list.

The static caravan on site at Sandy Bay in Porthcawl had been the first thing to go for the Foley's. It had been the focus of family holidays, weekend breaks and occasional jaunts for over a decade. He had bought it at a time when his wages reflected the hard and dangerous work he did underground. The caravan had been a little slice of local luxury, an oasis of calm and clear, crisp air in an otherwise desert of black and dusty coal. Michael had loved the caravan, so too had the kids, and Sian – after a while. Sian had always liked the finer things in life, not that she was born with a silver spoon in her mouth or anything like that. She had seemed to develop a taste for expensive holidays, clothes and cars as Michael's wages had increased with his experience underground. The pay had been good and Michael didn't have a problem with spending the money either. How times change.

Michael tinkered with the timing on a Fiesta XR2. At least he had the car repairs to fall back on. He had completed an apprenticeship as a mechanic prior to going down the mines at the age of twenty. Back then, the Coal Board offered a decent wage, more than he could get in the local garage, and there was a tidy pension for colliers too. The Union had worked hard over the years to secure the decent working conditions they had enjoyed up until the strike but now it looked like the personal feud between Thatcher and Scargill was destroying those hard won victories.

He adjusted the top-dead-centre on the timing and checked it with the strobe. All looked good. That was another thirty quid in the pocket. It wasn't much but it paid for his little bit of luxury, the only thing he had left.

Michael switched off the engine and hung the key on a hook with two other sets that belonged to cars waiting for his magic touch.

He dipped his hands into a tub of Swarfega and massaged the gel through his hands.

He could hear Sian playing her favourite music, it was loud and a tune he happened to like himself. Tina Turner wailed about her 'Private Dancer' and Michael almost laughed, had it not been so ironic. He thought about the kids. Things had not been good at home.

He wiped the oil from his hands with a cloth, switched off the overhead light and walked through the back door of the garage that led up a narrow path to the rear of the terraced house. A line of single-bulb lampposts in the rear lane cast enough light on the path for him to find his way to the back door.

The kids were staying down their grandmothers and Sian was getting ready for 'work.'

The back door was open and he kicked his oily boots into a corner and slipped his overalls off before climbing the narrow stairs to the bathroom on the first floor.

Sian was standing in the tiny aubergine coloured bathroom, applying her lipstick in the mirror.

She was already wearing her work clothes, a black leather jacket he had bought her for her thirtieth birthday over a white fitted blouse, a black leather skirt that didn't extend down past the top of her thighs and a pair of black leather boots that seemed to want to fill in the lack of leather between her knees and the hem of the skirt. She had bought the skirt and the boots from her first week in her new 'job.'

He could understand why she seemed to resent him. He had once been the breadwinner, the head of the family, but now he had to scrape for every penny and felt the humiliation daily, but he couldn't understand how she could do those things with other men. He had heard the excuses and the bitterness in her voice as she spat her reasons at him, but *she* could never understand how it made *him* feel. How could she sell herself to other men? Michael knew she was desperate for money, to return to the standard of living they had once enjoyed, but he had assured her he'd find a way to make the money. The little house had a decent sized garage at the bottom of the back garden and Michael had opened it up for auto repairs. It wasn't bringing in the same kind of money as before but at least it kept the wolf from the door for a while.

Sian had mocked him. She had told him that she earned more in an hour than he made in two days.

He watched her for a moment and saw her look at him through the reflection in the mirror. She forced a fake smile and began applying her eye shadow.   .

Michael turned away and pulled on a pair of jeans, a clean shirt and a heavy jumper. He slipped on his shoes and dropped back down the stairs. The keys to the old Marina were in the dish by the phone in the hallway and he snatched them as he left the house.

***

He checked the money Pete had given him for the work on the XR2 and tucked it into his pocked as he stopped the old Morris Marina outside the Maesteg Snooker hall. He could see the dark figure sitting in the sporty, two-tome green Capri opposite.

Michael checked around and stepped from the car.

Capri-man watched him as he approached and wound down the window. "Alright, Mike?"

Michael shrugged.

"Usual?"

Michael nodded.

"Let's see the colour of your money first, eh?"

Mike produced notes he'd just received from Pete and handed them to Capri-man.

Capri-man snorted derisively and took a small packet from inside his coat. "There you go."

Michael said nothing. He took the packet and tucked it into his trouser pocket as he walked back to his car.

PYE IN THE SKY

Present Day.

The dark blue Transit van trundled off the main road and bumped up along a rough track leading into the forestry. The van coughed and whined as it stayed in low gear to negotiate a gentle climb that would have been no challenge for a better maintained example of Ford's commercial workhorse.

Alan Pye found the clearing, a place he had visited many times before. He eased off the gas and swung the van between two trees and cut the engine. He sat quietly for a moment. The radio had not worked for months but he wasn't here to listen to music. He wound down the window and stuck his head out to check the immediate area. It was quiet, only the birds chirping in the trees and the distant sound of a small stream swollen by the recent heavy downpours. At least it wasn't raining now.

He opened the van door and stood by the side to relieve his bladder, keeping a wary eye out and listening for any vehicle that might be heading up the track to join him. He knew courting couples and druggies sometimes used the clearing but they pretty much kept themselves to themselves. Nobody would bother him.

He finished up his toiletries and climbed back into the van. It was getting dark but that was how he liked it. Although the clearing was not far from Maesteg Golf Club, as the crow flies, it was still far enough away to keep him secluded whilst he did the business.

He didn't want to run the engine to keep warm. He didn't have enough fuel for that. He climbed between the two front seats and stepped onto the soft, stained mattress on the floor of the rear cargo hold. A thick duvet was rolled into a corner and he pulled one end and arranged it to cover the mattress. He then clambered to the back doors and checked they were locked. Satisfied, he slid under the duvet and lay still, staring up at the star map he had taped to the metal ceiling. The map had tiny fluorescent dots to represent the constellations sometimes visible above the northern hemisphere. Alan Pye knew he hadn't had a chance to see many stars of late. The rain had been incessant and the sky shrouded in clouds.

He lay there, thinking about the stars, how he had always wanted to travel into space, to be an astronaut. He sneered at his crazy and unrealistic dream, it was never going to be a reality for Alan Pye from poxy Maesteg.

Having left the local Comprehensive school at sixteen with no qualifications, he had drifted into petty crime and into the clutches of the local drug dealer. It had all started off innocently enough, a little blow here and a line of coke there – whenever he could afford it, but he knew he had written his own fate the day he woke from his first fix of heroin. That one night of debauched fun had led him to this place, right here and right now. He thought of the local people who shunned him, the blokes he had played rugby with in school, the girls he had dated before he met the Fixer. Nobody wanted to be near him now. They all acted as though he was infectious or something. He knew he only had himself to blame. He knew it would never get better for him until he kicked the habit.

He raised himself off the mattress and clicked on the interior light. His gear was wrapped in a small plastic bag in a wooden box fixed to the wheel arch. He did the business and shot the fix into his arm. He dropped his gear back into the bag and lay back, thinking of his mother as he closed his eyes.

FLASHER

Sarah laughed at Julie's expression as she supped the sour sherbet from the yellow cardboard tube.

"Oh, that's sharp," said Julie.

Katie snatched the tube and dipped her finger into the white powder and shovelled a small pile into her mouth. "Mmm, I love sherbet."

The three girls giggled as they walked along the road leading to the sea front. They had made the walk to the fairground several times over the last few days but the sun had finally broken through the clouds for the first time since they arrived and patches of bright blue sky promised weather better than that forecast by the HTV weather girl.

"How much have you got on you?" Katie asked her friends.

"I've got a tenner," said Julie.

"Me too," agreed Sarah.

"I've got twelve-fifty. Won't do much with that lot, will we?" Katie sighed.

"We can have a few rides," Julie said. "Anyway, we've only got an hour before we have to be back at the caravan. Mam said she'd kill me if we're late."

Sarah and Julie had spent a few days with Katie at her parents' caravan in Trecco Bay. The weather had been a bit pants but at least they had enjoyed the time together.

The fair had been the main attraction for the girls. They loved the way the boys running the rides flirted with them, they loved that more than the rides themselves.

They took a well-used short cut between two long lines of caravans that snipped a couple of minutes off the walk.

"I hope that lush bloke is still on the bumpers," Katie said.

"He'll have kittens if he finds out you're only fourteen," Sarah warned.

"It's only a guide," Julie joked. "Anyway, nothing wrong with a bit of flirting. Can't get done for that, can you?"

"I don't like him. I think he's creepy," Sarah said. "Did you see the colour of his hands?"

Katie nudged her, "But he had a nice smile."

The girls laughed then froze.

A naked man stepped out from between two caravans, about a hundred yards ahead of them. He stood still and his odd looking face seemed expressionless as he held something in his hand that caused the girls to scream.

BACK TO THE OFFICE

It was my first day back in the office and boy had I been looking forward to it.

Molly was back home and recovering well, if truth be told, I was getting under her feet.

It had only been a couple of weeks and the break had done me good, batteries re-charged.

It was time to get down to business. The Ambrose and Nevin cases were finally closed. The Hulk had shit on his chips, good riddance - a DC with steroid abuse issues was not conducive to ethical policing.

Operation Hydra was a tremendous success, with the four banged up on remand and the squad finally firing on all cylinders.

Things in the garden were looking rosy.

Next on the agenda were the Leigh Delamere duo and the 'Flying Dutchman.' There was something niggling me in the back of my mind, I didn't know what it was, but I had this itch that I desperately wanted to scratch.

Everything had been on hold whilst I had been away on my break, neither Sussex nor the Customs had been informed of Hydra and that was the way I wanted it to stay.

Mind you, when they got to hear about it the shit would hit the fan, big time, but fuck Sussex and fuck the Customs, they seemed to like to treat us as bumbling country bumpkins and rarely shared information with us.

Mike had gathered all the relevant intelligence around the Hydra operation and were going to have a conference with the squad after lunch.

I just finished my second coffee of the morning when I received a call from our firearms department and I'm like a dog with two dicks. The Glock recovered from the hitman, Nevin, had been examined. The gun was recovered from the body of the Scottish psycho who tried to kill me.

He'd accepted a 'hit' on me set up by my former colleague Cliff Ambrose who I had locked up for murder and a few others things. Nevin, the hit man, had been dying from cancer at the time and it seems he had wanted to go out in a blaze of glory, to take out a copper before he spun off his mortal coil.

The Glock had been used in two murders in Glasgow and an armed robbery at an off licence where the gun was discharged. This was the icing on the cake. Two murders and an armed robbery cleared up, all whilst I was looking after the Mrs. Fuck me; this is what the job is all about.

I had visions of entertaining a few Jock cops for a couple of days.

I intended to inform Mike after lunch so he could liaise with our Celtic cousins about the Nevin shit, I had no doubt there would be a few drams in it for us.

It was great to be back, the future was bright. I could feel it.

THE TWO TURKS

Later that afternoon, the whole squad turned up at the office for the briefing.

It was great to see them all laughing and joking and full of a renewed confidence - on top of their game - a totally different attitude to a few weeks ago when I met them for the first time.

"It's great to have you back boss, you and Mike have transformed the squad, we have direction and purpose now and we are behind you a hundred-and-ten per cent," Steve Thompson, my D.S. said. "By the way give Molly our best wishes."

I thanked Steve and the squad for the commitment and professionalism they all showed during Hydra. "Hopefully, this squad will now go from strength to strength. I'm proud of you all." I told them honestly. "Now back to business. Over to you Mike."

Mike was my DI and had been running things whilst I'd been away. He came to the squad with me and was as straight as they come. "Right ladies and gent's, this is where we are at the moment. We made the ènquiry with the Met' about the van that was sighted at Leigh Delamere with the Barry team of villains. It was registered to a restaurant in Camden, but was subsequently sold on through the auctions. The current owners are a pair of brothers from Hastings, Sussex. Both are of Turkish origin and run the Pizza and Kebab takeaway in Havelock Road in Hastings. They've been resident in the UK for the last five years and their details are as follows.

"Adil BINICI. Born 1.8.1990. No Pre Cons.

"Dalan BINICI. Born 8.8.1992. No Pre Cons

"Both live together in a flat above the takeaway. We are in possession of up-to-date photographs of the pair, please don't ask how we got them, but I would like to thank Jane for that stick of rock she brought back from Brighton." The team laughed. Mike continued, "There is no doubt that these are the two men who off-loaded the five boxes containing the coke at Leigh Delamere. That's as far as we've gone at the minute, the enquiry will obviously have to be taken forward. I think the boss will fill you in on that."

I stood to take the floor. "Well, what do you reckon, ladies and gents, what have we got, any suggestions?"

"It's got to be importation boss," Colin Anderson offered, "from the continent, I reckon. Either coming in by boat or light aircraft? There are loads of small beaches and airfields along the coast that are not monitored. Ideal, I reckon, to bring it in. If that's the case, we'll have to hand it over."

I nodded. "Totally agree with you, Col.' That was my theory. As for handing the case over? Well, that's another matter we'll address when and if the time is right. Anyway, I have a meeting with the ACC later and I'll put the theory to him and tell him the way forward." The group sniggered. They had come to know that the ACC pretty much did as I suggested. He trusted me; at least he did before my recent meltdown. I hoped the relationship hadn't changed.

"Before you all go," I added, holding up my hand for silence, "anything from the four on remand?"

"No, nothing, boss," Colin said. "No comment in interviews all the way through. In my opinion, I reckon Dean is the main-man there, bit more articulate than the other three and probably the negotiator with the two Turks."

Colin looked around at the squad and I could see from their facial expressions and body language they were in agreement with him.

I nodded my head. I was pleased they were all singing off the same hymn sheet.

"Okay everybody, knock off early for the day and thank you all very much. I'll let you all know the outcome with the ACC and, hopefully, we can take it forward, either on our own or with joint cooperation with H.M. Customs and Sussex."

SHOCK AND ANGER

Caroline watched the three girls through the open door as they sat quietly in the interview room of Porthcawl Police Station. She could see they were clearly in a state of shock. The father of one of the girls stood alongside her and was close to spitting bullets. He'd demanded answers that Caroline couldn't provide.

W.P.C. Caroline Williams had been lumbered with the 'Dick of the Dunes' – as the flasher had become known within the confines of the station – and had taken every step she could to bring him to justice. She had even recovered a soiled tissue from a personal encounter with the flasher and now had his DNA profile on file. But nobody could give her a name for the bastard. He had no criminal record that had required the collection of a DNA sample. She had a poor quality image of the man's face but there was something really strange about it. It seemed to lack any kind of animation, of life. She was beginning to think it might be a mask? That would fit in with a comment from one of the girls who said she thought the flasher looked like someone off the telly.

Terry McGuire had secured an aide for Caroline on the local CID and she had kept the flasher file. She was determined to bring him to book.

"So what are you going to do about it?"

"I've already told you, Mr Morgan, we're working on it and…"

"Working on it? I heard from people on the caravan site that you've had this nutter running around for months."

Caroline nodded. "Yes. It's proving to be a nuisance..."

"It's more than a nuisance," he fumed, "it's a serious matter when three fourteen year old girls are exposed to that sort of…that sort of…perversion."

"I agree, Mr Morgan, I totally agree with you and all I can do is try and assure you that we're taking the matter very seriously." Caroline fully understood the man's concerns. She too wanted to catch the bastard but she knew the will to solve the case within the station wasn't exactly what she had told Morgan it was. She knew they could wrap it all up quickly if the divisional superintendent allocated more officers and resources to it.

"I'll take statements off the girls, individually, and then I'll have a word with my DS on CID. I promise you that I'll still be working on the case and I'll let you know as soon as there are any developments.

That seemed to do the trick. Mr Morgan joined the girls in the interview room and explained to them what Caroline would do next.

It was going to be another long day and the flasher was now getting to be a real pain in the arse.

BODY IN THE VAN

Jeff took the call from the Op's Room; the uniform boys had found a young lad's body in a van in the forestry opposite the Maesteg Golf Club.

The information was that he'd been missing for a few days and that his death was possibly drug related.

The only member of the team I had in the office, other than Jeff, was Jane, "I'll get up there boss," she offered.

"Cracking," I said, "but leave the bike, I'll drive you."

I told Jeff to get a message to the officer at the scene not to touch anything, and we'd be there in twenty minutes.

"SOCO and the Police Surgeon are on their way, boss," he told me.

There had been many occasions throughout my career when vital evidence had been compromised, either by sheer stupidity or just plain laziness, I didn't want this to be one of those times.

On the way up the valley, Jane and I started chatting, she was a sharp cookie, qualified to sergeant, but not really interested in promotion as she loved being part of the squad.

Even though I had only known her a few weeks, I could see a lot of potential in Jane and I thought I'd encourage her to look at the broader picture regarding promotion. She clearly didn't like to talk about herself but she did tell me that she had a son. From what I could gather, things were difficult between her and her ex-partner. The Force needed Sergeants with drive and initiative, the supervision these days had become pretty dire and, little did I know at that time, we would get a prime example of this shortly.

We arrived at the forestry gate and drove in for about a mile, then turned left onto a rough track. It had obviously been well used over time; I was thinking of courting couples, druggies or maybe both?

We arrived at the scene. The only officers present were a young PC by the name of Haydn Roberts, a local boy who would give me chapter and verse on the dead lad. My old muckers, the Police Surgeon, Dr Hugo Faulkner and DS Glyn Walcott a top-notch Scenes of Crime Officer were huddled around the van.

The van was an old, blue Ford Transit and we walked to the open back door to see the young lad lying peacefully in the back on an old mattress. He was pale and his skin had a blue-yellow tinge, I could see the drug paraphernalia in a bag and he still had his belt tied tightly just above it. He must have had quite a hit to die like that, I thought.

Dr Hugo Faulkner joined us, "I've had a quick look at him, Terry. Looks like an overdose. Been dead...I would say...er...twenty-four to thirty-six hours. The P.M. will tell us more."

"Not like our 'ice man' then, Doc?" I reminded him. "Five fucking years..." We both chuckled.

"Thank you, Doc," I said as I turned to Glyn. "Have you got anything?"

"Well, I got the spoon and the lighter, Ter,' they were alongside him, and I found a small bag of powder in his jeans pocket. I was just about to do the syringe and belt when you arrived. I've photographed everything in situ' and I'll get all the exhibits off to the lab' later today. We should have the results in a couple of days. I'm not pre-empting the result, but I think it's a heroin overdose that's done for the poor kid."

I turned to PC Roberts, "It's your turn now, son. What can you tell me?"

The PC pulled his pocket book from his coat and flipped it open. "His name is Alan Pye. He's twenty years of age and lives on the Blaencaerau Estate with his mum. Sir, he's been missing for a few days, his mum reported him because she was concerned. He hadn't come home and that was out of character."

I nodded sadly, wondering what the poor woman would say and do when she found out her boy was dead. As a parent, I couldn't think of any news that could be worse. "Anything else?"

"Yes. He's got a bit of form for Taking Without Consent, Possession and Burglary. I know him quite well, he wasn't a bad kid, just got in with a few wrong 'uns, you know what it's like, Sir."

"Oh yes, Haydn. I know only too fucking well what it's like."

In fairness, PC Haydn Roberts offered to inform the family. "I'll go and break the bad news to his mum and do all the relevant statements."

Nice to see somebody with a bit of shape about them, I thought. Then I realised that he was on his own. "Where's your Inspector and Sergeant?"

"They're in a PACT meeting in the Town Hall, sir."

"In a fucking PACT meeting?" I said, astonished. "We've got a young man dead as a fucking dodo, not half a mile away from the nick and they're in a fucking PACT meeting? Give me fucking strength."

I felt sorry for Haydn. It wasn't fair to dump it all on him. "Look, you go with Jane and see the mother, break the news to her and make sure that she's okay," I said. "You can do the ID with mum tomorrow down at the mortuary...after the PM."

I took Jane aside. "Jane, give Haydn a hand, just make sure everything is okay. I'll hang on for the undertaker and once they've taken the body I'll secure the van. It can be picked up later. I'll meet you back at the Maesteg nick."

"No problem, boss, we'll sort it."

I only had to wait another fifteen minutes before the undertakers arrived. I gave them all the details they needed and they removed poor Alan from the back of the van and placed him gently into a black zip up body bag. I will say one thing for the undertakers, they treated young Alan with dignity, very professional, and I liked that. I've never seen this crew of undertakers acting with anything other than the greatest respect to the unfortunate souls they collected for me. That was nice to see. It's common knowledge that emergency service personnel have a reputation for having a weird sense of humour but, in all fairness, when it came to stuff like this we all had the certain knowledge that we too would one day end up being taken away. No matter how many times in your career you see this it still saddens you, especially if it's a youngster being loaded into the back of the undertakers van.

I then secured the vehicle and made my way to the nick.

My next job was to update the Inspector and Sergeant about the incident and, by fuck, I was looking forward to that.

I arrived at the nick, it was quiet and I made my way to the Inspector's office, I knocked the door and they were in there, the pair of fuckers, drinking coffee.

I identified myself to them, as they didn't know me from Adam. I didn't bother to sit down. It wasn't a social call.

"Well, gent's," I began. "You've got a twenty year old miss- per called Alan Pye dead as a fucking dodo up in the forestry, looks like an overdose of heroin. How did the PACT meeting go?"

The Inspector and sergeant looked flustered. I threw the van keys onto the desk and said, "The young lad's van, it's still in the forestry. SOCO have finished with it, just have it collected and stored, if you've got the time that is?"

They didn't answer me. I could see they knew what I thought of them. It was best they kept quiet.

I told them that a member of my squad would liaise with young Haydn Roberts down at the mortuary tomorrow to top and tail it for the Coroner. I turned about face and left the room, I was disgusted with the pair of them. PACT meeting taking precedence over a serious incident, what the fuck is that all about?

I made my way to the charge room just as young Roberts and Jane arrived.

I told Roberts that he had done well, and that Jane would meet him down the mortuary tomorrow for the PM and Identification.

He looked pleased with himself – he had a right to. "I'll get Alan's Mum down there for about two pm, will that be okay, sir?"

"Yes, no problem with that, I've cleared it with 'Blues Brothers' upstairs." I know I was disrespecting senior officers in front of a PC, but that's me, fuck the pair of them. They didn't deserve the respect of junior officers. How could they leave a young PC to deal with that on his own? In fairness, he impressed me and that made me feel good.

DIFFERENT STROKES

The well-dressed man sauntered through the bar in the centre of Cardiff. The city was buzzing. The Stereophonics had finished their gig in the Principality Stadium a little after ten-thirty and the thirty-thousand or so revellers were either queuing to leave via the bus or train station or filling all the drinking establishments to capacity.

Dressed in blue leather trousers, a matching leather vest and jacket that looked as expensive as it cost, Rod' felt good. A line of coke and several gins had him in a good frame of mind. Work had been a drag but it also had its advantages. He'd made contacts through his clients that he would otherwise never have encountered.

The bar was full of men and he believed all were his soul-mates. He could feel the eyes of some of the men follow him as he stepped up to the bar and produce a large denomination note to buy two more drinks.

Although he was overweight and accepted that he'd passed his sell-buy date, Rod' could still pull someone for a night of fun. None of the clientele present was his type though. The bar had begun to lose its appeal to him. The customers seemed to be somewhere around his age and that wasn't good enough for him. Why settle for mutton when you could have lamb? That's what he liked to say to those who were privy to his tastes.

The barman took his order and Rod' squeezed through the milling crowd back to a small but high table pushed into a corner near the door.

The jukebox music changed to "It's Raining Men," by the Weathergirls and those standing in the middle of the bar began jumping and singing along with the popular song.

Rod' reached the table and placed the drinks down in front of a young girl Rod' had met in work nearly a year earlier.

Alice Harris looked older than she actually was. Standing a little over five-seven, she had perfected the art of the flawless complexion through careful management of her skin and with the help of Rod's generous wallet.. Her thick black hair was cropped short and gelled into spikes on top.

Rod' could see the lines of mascara she used to emphasise her deep green eyes and he couldn't wait to take her home and get a closer look at those pools of jade. He knew the eye colour was the result of fancy contact lenses, but Rod' didn't care. He wasn't really interested in her eyes, if truth be told.

Nobody bothered them, Rod' was a regular customer and everyone knew him. They knew he was a wealthy and powerful man. Nobody would ever question his motives with a girl who had just turned sixteen.

CONFERENCE WITH THE ACC

After Jane and I had got back to the office, I tasked Jeff with trawling through any intelligence on drug related deaths within the Force area during the last six months.

I knew there weren't many, but seeing young Alan Pye with that needle in his arm set my mind thinking.

About ten years ago, when I was a Divisional DS in Pontypridd, youngsters were overdosing and dropping like flies throughout the valley. It had been down to a batch of heroin that was almost 100 per cent pure.

The poor bastards were injecting something like six-times their normal dose; their bodies couldn't take it. We were finding them everywhere, stairwells of flats, in between shop dumpsters and in abandoned buildings. I think there were about five in total. Young kids, dying in filth, not a pretty sight, I can tell you.

I just hoped that young Pye was going to be an isolated case.

After tasking Jeff, I rang to fix an appointment with the ACC, and I was told to get down to HQ as soon as possible.

When I got there, it was the usual bollocks, "Come on in Terry, how's it all going, how are the squad?" I'm being a bit harsh, the ACC's a good bloke and he usually let me have full reins – that's all I could ever ask for.

"Everything's tickety-boo, boss. Going well, the team are chomping at the bit, fair play. Hydra has given them a new lease of life." Hydra was the operational name for the drugs bust we had recently successfully pulled off. There were a few loose ends that I wanted to tie.

"I suppose it's Hydra you want to discuss then, Terry?" he said with a wry smile.

He's a sharp bastard fair play.

"Cut to the chase, Terry, the way forward, any plans?"

"Well, boss, my theory is that the two Turks from Hastings are obviously heavily involved with the importation of Cocaine from the continent. They're ideally placed on the coast, it's just a matter of putting all of the pieces together."

"We'll have to involve all the relevant agencies, Interpol, Customs, SOCA and obviously Sussex, do you see any problem with that?" the ACC asked.

I had to agree with the ACC to be fair, this was going to be a massive operation - on both sides of the Channel, I reckoned. All our intelligence would have to be shared. I had no problem with that, but I also wanted my squad involved.

The ACC nodded. "I'll set up a conference at HQ with all the agencies within the next few days. How do you feel about us seconding a DS and four DC's to whatever operation there is in this in the future?"

"I always knew the time would come when we'd have to hand over Hydra to the other agencies and Sussex," I agreed.

As much as it fucking narked me, I had to let it go, there was too much at stake, today this had become International.

"As for losing five of the squad? I see no problem with that," I said. "It still leaves me with a DS and fifteen...more than enough to cope."

I got back to the office around six. Jeff was still there at his desk. He looked knackered.

"Why don't you fuck off home, Jeff?"

"I just want to fill you in on the drug related deaths, boss."

"Fine ," I said.

"Well, there has only been five, boss. One in Bridgend, one in Swansea, one in Porthcawl and two in Cardiff. None of them were as a result of intravenous injection. All were cocaine or amphetamine related. The young lad, PYE is the first by needle for a fair while."

I thanked Jeff and told him to go home.

I entered my office and walked slalom around the stacks of case files littering the office floor to my chair. I poured myself a coffee, sat back in my chair and pondered the day's activities.

I then gave Molly a ring and asked her to get the supper on.

***

I had a hell of a surprise when I got home. I heard voices as I opened the front door and then I heard Molly laughing and the deeper, sonorous tones of a man whispering something. The voices were coming from our bedroom.

I could feel my stomach tighten, a feeling of dread that I had never expected to experience with my Molly. She had a man in the bedroom with her.

I crept up the stairs, not knowing why or what I would do if my growing fears were realised. I stopped on the top step and listened. The male's voice was louder now, joking with my wife.

Then I smiled and felt the tension drain from me like a plug being pulled from a bath tub. I opened the door to our bedroom to find my son, Christian sitting at the bottom of Molly's bed.

He turned from his mother and smiled at me. He stood and we embraced. I hadn't seen my son in nearly a year. He had moved to Hong Kong two years ago to work on construction projects with his engineering firm. Molly and I had visited him just once in that time. Work and finances made it impossible for us to travel as much as we both would have liked.

"Hi, dad."

"Hi, son. What a surprise!"

"Got a few days leave. Thought I'd take the opportunity to come and check on mam."

Molly was grinning like she'd just won the lottery. "Sorry, love. Didn't feel too good, so came to bed early then Chris arrived. Haven't had time to make dinner. Perhaps you can get us all some chips?

I smiled, kissed Molly then cwtched my son again – can't have too many hugs. "I told you not to bother coming. Must have cost you a fortune and you're mam's as tough as old boots."

"Thanks very much," Molly said, feigning insult.

"I can see she's on the mend," Chris said. "What the hell happened, dad?"

"Your mother hasn't told you?"

"She said, 'ask your dad,' just like you used to say 'ask your mam' whenever I asked something you didn't want to answer."

I sniggered. It was true, especially where the awkward questions had arisen around sex. "Sit down," I said. "I'll make us some tea and we'll have a chat about it over a nice cuppa."

I bounced down the stairs and into our small and dated kitchen. Molly had been on to me to change it, to extend the house and put in new units, but I didn't see the point in wasting the little spare money we had on a larger kitchen when there was only the two of us now. The irony of life wasn't lost on me. You need the space when the children are at home but tend not to be able to afford it. When you're older, and the kids have left home, you tend to have a little more money set aside but no need for the extra space. Life is arse-backwards.

I made a pot of tea as Chris clumped down the stairs and joined me at a stool on the breakfast bar. "Great to see you both," he said.

"You should have told us," I said. "I'd have picked you up from the airport."

"Wanted to surprise you."

"You did that. How did you get from the airport?"

"Taxi."

"That must have cost you a fortune?"

He smiled. "I can afford it, dad."

"Business going well, then?"

"The contract I told you about has been given the green light. It'll make us, dad."

I grinned. My son had done well for himself. He'd been pretty focussed since he was a kid, always playing with construction sets and building things out of leftover bits and bobs. By the age of thirteen he could dismantle a computer, install new hardware and software. He had achieved excellent grades in school and a first in engineering. That secured him a job with a multi-national company that took him to Hong Kong. Within a year he had impressed enough to be offered a partnership. I was incredibly proud of him and his sister.

"How's Carmen, have you spoken?" Carmen is my daughter and she moved to Australia about the same time Chris moved to Hong Kong. We lost both kids from our everyday lives in a space of a couple of months. She worked for a university doing some kind of environmental research.

"She's relieved that mam's okay," Chris said. "Her job seems fine and she told me she's buying her own place."

"Prices are higher in Australia," I said.

"She seems to be doing well. She wanted to come home to see mam."

"I talked her out of it."

"Don't be surprised if she turns up soon."

"Do you know something we don't," I grinned.

"Nah. Just know what she's like."

I sipped my tea and noticed that Chris hadn't touched his. "Don't waste a good tea bag," I said.

Chris looked distracted.

"What's up? You're mam will be okay."

He nodded. "Came as a hell of a shock, dad. What the hell happened?"

"It's a long story…"

"I've got time."

I wondered if I should keep the truth from him, to save him some worry, but I knew he'd find out sooner or later. "Some bloke I locked up, a former colleague, a Chief Inspector…"

"You arrested a colleague?" he interrupted.

"I had no choice. It was two, actually. A DI and a DCI. Both were corrupt bastards and one had killed a druggie."

"Fuck!"

That surprised me from Chris. He had never sworn in front of me before and I had never sworn in front of him. I kept all the swearing for work. This would be my first exception to the long-standing rule. "Fuck, is right," I said, feeling immediately embarrassed about my lapse. "Anyway, the DCI wanted to get his own back on me and found some crazy-arsed Jock with a few months left to live...dying of cancer. He took a contract on me and mam nearly paid the price."

"Bloody hell, dad. That's serious stuff."

I nodded.

"It's time you retired, dad. Spend time with mam, while you can."

I nodded but he knew I couldn't do it.

"Seriously, dad, you can't change the world."

"I know. But I can make small changes, here and there, small changes that make a difference to the small people."

He shrugged. "You've done enough, dad. Spend time with mam and let her spend time with you. Let someone else take the reins. If you counted up the time you've been together I reckon you've only been married for about ten years."

I had to agree. "More like five. Missed you all growing up. That annoys me the most. Missed the best part of your childhood."

He shrugged. "I resented it at the time but I knew you were doing something important. Didn't make it easier though."

I knew he was right. "I resent losing those times. I resent it but someone had to do it."

"Did it really have to be you, dad?"

I couldn't answer. I knew it *did* have to be me. It's just the way I am. I've never been able to stand back and watch people get hurt. I guess I hadn't thought of the hurt I had caused to my own family in the process.

"Anyway, how's life out there for you?" I said, hoping to change the subject.

"It's, er, complicated."

My interest was piqued. "Oh? In what way?"

"I've got a girlfriend."

I grinned. "That's great. Is she from Hong Kong?"

"No, she's actually from Hertfordshire. She works in the office."

"What's her name, are you going to bring her to meet us?"

He nodded slowly. "I suppose we'll have to do something soon. The baby will be here in about six months."

I think most of my tea went over the counter top.

CLEAN UP

The young woman fished for the keys to the building. They should have been easy to find, they were on a large oval iron ring the size of Mick Jagger's gob. She sniggered at the thought of having Mick Jagger in her bag. She loved the Stones. She had listened to them on the radio her father had swopped for some gardening work when she was not much older than seven or eight. The Stones weren't the type of band a girl like her would normally have been listening to. Beyoncé and Lady Ga Ga, even Madonna, was more to the liking of her friends. Perhaps it was the connection with her dad? She stopped and breathed deeply. She had that empty feeling of loss again, something she always experienced when she thought of her father.

The security officer usually let her in but he wasn't answering the bell. Probably doing the rounds in the other parts of the building. No problem. She shook her bag and could hear the rattle of the keys somewhere amongst the mess she carried everywhere these days. The bag was large and had a screen-printed logo of a superstore and two long canvas handles. The keys lay beneath a small plastic Tupperware lunch box.

The key opened the door and she dropped the bag inside and rushed to the alarm control panel to key in the code she had been given. It was an easy one to remember. The alarm beeped twice as it went into sleep mode and the woman retrieved her bag and locked the door behind her. The alarm for the door was always set when the security guard was elsewhere.

A marble-clad reception area led off to a series of offices, six in all, that she was contracted to clean each evening between the hours of six and eight. The job took just under ninety minutes, if the security guard left her alone. He loved to talk, probably helped to break the boredom, but she would still get paid for two hours and this was the only job she had on her schedule for the night.

Opening the broom cupboard, she filled her wheelie-bucket with warm water, added the detergent and mopped down the reception area before dragging a silly-faced vacuum cleaner across the cheap carpets of the six offices.

She checked her watch. She'd finished in a little over an hour. That gave her an hour for herself.

The gent's toilet was another shrine to expensive marble tiles and fancy soap dispensers. Three cubicles were built into one wall and she carried her shopping bag into the last in the line.

Sitting on the closed seat, she took the Tupperware box from the bag and peeled the lid. Inside was a syringe, a spoon, a lighter and a silver paper packet.

ZIRCON INSURANCE COMPANY

Molly was over the moon last night. Together with Chris, we necked our fish and chips straight from the newspaper and washed it down with a glass of white.

We laughed and joked, it was like the old days. Molly was on the mend, both physically and mentally. She was in a good place after all the shit she had gone through.

As for me? Well, as long as Molly's happy, so am I. I was so pleased to see Chris but the news of the baby had really taken me by surprise. I didn't even have a clue that he had a young lady. After the initial shock, we talked it through and Chris assured me that he intended to play a major part in the baby's life but that they had no intention of tying the knot just yet.

Molly was over the moon at the news. This surprised me as she had always been against the idea of having a child out of wedlock. Oh how times change.

I drove to work with a smile on my face. Happy days, especially since the hours I've been working have not been too bad; conducive to a stable relationship at last.

***

I got into the office early and Jeff was already there. He had taken to office management like a duck to water. He was becoming known as 'the font of all knowledge' within the squad, he had the ear of everyone.

It was a quiet sort of morning; a few of the squad were in doing paperwork and a few had gone out to do a bit of surveillance work on foot. Mad-keen they were.

Then, at about midday, Jeff received yet another call about a drug related death, this time at the Zircon Insurance Building on Station Hill in Bridgend.

The only information we had was that a young female cleaner had been found dead in the gent's toilet.

I tasked Churchy and Jane to attend, telling them to keep me updated.

*∗∗

Churchy and Jane arrived to find that the body of the young woman had already been removed to the mortuary at the Princess of Wales Hospital; the only copper left at the scene was a local DC by the name of Peter Harding.

"What's the score?" Churchy asked.

"The young woman was a cleaner by the name of Leanne Morgan," Harding said. "Apparently, the alarm record shows that Leanne had entered to clean the offices at around six pm last night, the on duty security officer had the rest of the building to check but knew she had entered because he has an alarm de-activation signal sent to his mobile when the cleaner comes in. He said he normally had a chat to her but there was a dodgy lock on the rear of the building and he'd been told to stay there for most of the night. He said he thought she had left the building later that night, even though she hadn't reset the alarm. He checked the ground floor, called for her and checked the ladies room, in case she was in there, but when he could find her he didn't think any more of it. He reset the door alarm and returned to his point.

"He was relieved from duty at eight this morning and that's when Leanne's body was found, slumped in the male toilets. They found her in one of the cubicles; she'd been shooting up, by the looks of it, all the gear was there beside her."

The Police surgeon had already been and gone. Churchy didn't expect anything different; they tend not to hang around if things look straightforward.

"I take it the scene has been photographed and all the exhibits collected?" Jane said.

Harding replied, "Yes. The SOCO boy did the business there, but he had another call and had to shoot off."

"Has the family been notified?" Jane enquired.

"As far as I know she has no relatives, lives alone in a bed sit up on Park Street by all accounts," Harding explained.

"And the address?" Churchy asked.

"Bryntirion," Harding said, confidently.

"Do you know it?"

"Yes it's an old Victorian House, all sorts living there, I know the landlord pretty well, we're always nicking someone or other from there. The landlord's got about ten rooms that he rents out."

"Well, I think that's our next port of call," Churchy said. "You can come along and introduce us to the landlord, Pete. By the way, what's his name?"

"Horace Brean. Been there for years."

"Has he got any form, Pete?"

"Aye, a few bits and pieces, a couple of indecent assaults going back about fifteen years. He was left the house and he's more or less a recluse there now, making a good living on the rents, keeping his nose clean. Mind you, the place is like a shit-house, he's got the ground floor flat, always in the window, you'll see him when we get there. He's like a fucking praying mantis."

They leave the security guard to shut up behind them and take the pool car to Park Street and pull up outside "Bryntirion," a large three-story Victorian house looking a bit tired and in need of a bit of loving care and attention.

"If this is what it's like outside, what's it like inside?" Churchy grumbled.

They made their way up the long narrow drive to the front door, and there was Brean the landlord, perched in the front window, just as Pete Harding as said.

They didn't have to knock, Brean was at the door quicker than a ferret up a trouser leg.

The landlord looked odd, short of stature and overweight, heavy stubble, thinning on top, with a permanently affixed, leering smile and spots of white spittle in the corners of his mouth. He wore a grey vest, covered in ash, grey jogging bottoms that had once probably been white and black lace up shoes.

"Fuck me," Churchy whispered, "what have we got here?"

Churchy produced his warrant card and made the introductions to Brean.

The landlord looked worried. "What do you want with me?"

Jane smiled reassuringly, We'd just like to have a look in Leanne Wood's room." She noticed the little man's eyes slowly appraising her from head to feet and back up again. She felt herself shiver.

"What's she done, been nicked has she?" he finally said as his eyes returned to her own.

Jane replied, "No, Mr Brean, she's dead."

Brean's expression changed, it morphed from smug to genuine shock.

Jane clocked it. There was also something else in his demeanour that she couldn't quite read.

Brean invited them in and took them through to Leanne's room; it was on the ground floor at the back of the house.

"Can you open it up for us please?" she said.

Brean pulled out a chain from his pocket with several Yale-type keys hanging from it.

He had no trouble selecting the right key and inserted into the lock of the door. Jane clocked this too. How did he know which key to use so easily?

"Thank you, Mr Brean, that will be all for now," she said.

Brean clearly didn't want to leave, "Would you like me to help?"

Jane put her hand on his shoulder, turned him away and ushered him along the corridor, "No, I think we can cope." He turned back in an attempt to follow but Jane shut the door on him and involuntarily wiped her hand on her trousers.

The room was tiny; there was a small single bed, a bedside cabinet and a wardrobe.

There was no carpet on the floor and there were no windows, it was more like a cell than a bed-sit room.

Jane put the light on and she and Churchy began to make a search.

Although sparse, Leanne had kept it clean and tidy. Everything was orderly.

There was a small bible on the bedside cabinet and a wooden crucifix hanging on the wall above the bed.

"Do you think Leanne was somewhat religious?" she said.

"Nah, Churchy replied. "Lots of these places have Bibles and things like that as part and parcel of the fixtures and fittings. Makes them appear respectable."

The initial search revealed nothing, but Jane wasn't happy. She sat on the bed and scanned the room.

Not many places to hide things. There was the wardrobe and the bedside cabinet. She asked Churchy to tip the bedside cabinet onto its side.

Churchy placed the Bible on the bed and did what Jane asked.

Taped to the underneath were two small syringes and a small plastic bag containing white powder. Churchy grinned. The items were bagged and tagged.

Jane let Churchy deal with the evidence. She sat back against the headboard and opened the Bible. Inside the front cover was a hand-written inscription *"Rosanna Balcoff 2014"*.

Jane put the Bible back on the cabinet and they left the room with the evidence and clicked the door lock to secure the room.

Brean was hovering at the front door, nervously puffing on a cigarette.

"How long has Leanne been living here?" Churchy asked.

"About three months," Brean said between frantic puffs. "Leanne kept herself to herself and only left her room to go to work as a cleaner down in Bridgend."

"Was she a good tenant?" Jane asked.

He nodded, flicked his stub out through the open door and fished for another from a soft-pack of Marlboro's. "Leanne paid her rent on time every Friday and ate in the communal kitchen."

"Any other women renting?" Churchy asked.

Brean lit the end of another cigarette, took a long drag and blew the smoke out through the door. "No, only Leanne," he finally coughed and spluttered.

"You need to leave them alone," Churchy nodded at the cigarette.

"Easier said than done," Brean sighed. "Pressure of being an entrepreneur." Churchy and Jane stifled a laugh.

"Did she have any male visitors at all?" Jane asked.

"No, only the bloke who came with her on the first visit…when she came to see the room."

"Do you know him, Mr Brean?"

"No, sorry, you know what it's like, hear no evil, see evil," he tapped his nose with his finger as if it was needed to emphasise his point.

"Thank you, Mr Brean. Keep that bedroom secure, we may be back," Churchy warned.

"No problem, officer. No problem at all."

Peter, the local DC, had been as much use as a colander condom. He dropped his cigarette as Jane and Churchy walked back to the car and fell in behind.

Jane and Churchy dropped Peter off at the nick and then made their way to the SOC Office with the powder and syringes.

Glyn Walcott ensured them that he'd have the items in the lab before close of play.

***

Jane and Churchy sat in the chairs opposite my desk, crammed in between the stacks of files that littered the floor. I really had to sort those files out soon.

They brought me up to speed with Leanne's sad demise and it saddened me. It was no way for a young girl to die.

I thanked Jane and Churchy for a job well done and then called Jeff into the office. He was beginning to remind me of Batman's butler. Indeed, he looked a lot like Michael Caine in that role, only considerable less fit. He really had to lose some weight.

"Jeff, I want you to put out an express message to all Divisions, something like…

"ANY DRUG RELATED DEATHS ARE TO BE REPORTED IMMEDIATELY TO THE DRUG SQUAD AND SCENES OF CRIME. THE BODIES ARE TO BE LEFT IN SITUE AND NO EXHIBITS ARE TO BE MOVED UNTIL A DRUG SQUAD DETECTIVE IS AT THE SCENE."

"No problem, boss, I'll sort it straight away."

I had a vision of Jeff, Batman's butler telling me, 'the Batmobile is ready, Master Wayne.'

I sniggered to myself then gave Mike a shout and told him to brief the squad about my pending circulation, reinforcing the need for one of our squad had to attend the scene if we gat a call.

"I have a terrible feeling of Déjà vu regarding these latest deaths. I just hope it is not a repeat of Ponty' again."

POST MORTEM

I had tasked Jane and Churchy to attend Leanne's post-mortem.

Doc' Stratford the local pathologist was going to do the business. I knew the Doctor very well; he'd carried out many PMs for me in sudden death cases. He was old school, should have been a Home Office Pathologist, but never actually wanted it. Don't think he liked the thought of the responsibility. But he was good. He would always give it to you straight and God forbid if you didn't furnish him with all the relevant information. He wasn't just good, he was top-notch, never missed a trick because he was so thorough.

I had spoken to him earlier that morning on the phone and brought him up to speed on the two deaths.

He had already carried out the PM on young Pye. It was a no brainer, massive overdose of opiates, however, he told me he didn't think he had been a regular user.

I had a feeling that Leanne may have overdosed on the same shit as young Pye.

Doc' Stratford promised me that he would move Leanne up the queue and do her first. He was always true to his word.

***

Before Churchy and Jane had arrived, the Doc' had nearly finished his business.

"Morning, officers," he said, "Terry has filled me in already with the gruesome details, it's your second in a couple of days isn't it? I hope it's not catching.

"Anyway, I've examined the deceased and I'd describe her as being a well-nourished female, aged between twenty and twenty-five, definitely sexually active, and most certainly a drug user, you can see by the track marks on both arms. Her teeth are in very good condition, no fillings and, by the way, definitely Eastern European."

Jane and Churchy looked at each other in surprise, "Doc,' you're telling us she's not British?" Jane said.

"Definitely eastern European, I would say, probably Polish, in fact, I'd bet my pension on it. As for cause of death? Again, I would say a drug overdose, but until I get the tox' report, I'm not betting on that one."

"We assumed she was local Doc' and with the name Leanne Morgan I thought she was well Welsh," Churchy said.

"One must never 'assume,' officers, get the full facts, a lesson learnt, I have no doubt? Tell Terry, I'll give him a ring later on with the definite cause, is there anything else? As you can see, I have them stacking up here and I really need to get on."

Churchy and Jane thanked the Doc' and returned to the office.

***

"Polish?" I asked.

Jane nodded. "Most likely, boss. Makes sense, too. There was a Bible in the woman's room with the name 'Rosanna Balcoff' written inside, might be her real name?"

"Well, don't just sit there, get back up to that twat Brean's house and get the Bible. Then get hold of DS Aled Powell on Special Branch, down at the Airport. Give him the information and see what he can do with the Immigration boys, it's a long shot but you never know.

"Oh, and by the way," I added, "get back to Zircon and find out the chapter and verse on Leanne – or whatever her name is -, you know the drill."

LEONARDO

Gethin and Janice Lewis parked their convertible M3 outside the Trecco Bay site office and collected the keys to their caravan. They made use of the site rental service for the periods they couldn't use it, and left the keys at reception. The rental service commission was expensive but convenient for them. They paid a little extra to ensure the customers were vetted. They didn't want their pride and joy destroyed by pissed up kids on a stag weekend from Splott.

It was rare for the Jones' to stay during February but they had contracted a local carpenter to repair some broken spindles on the decking guardrail and thought an overnighter would be a welcome break. Gethin left the M3 at reception, he knew the carpenter's van would need the parking space outside the van, and they walked the half-mile or so to their secluded spot in the enormous park.

Having switched on the heating and turned back the bed covers, Gethin and Barbara slumped into the settee and switched on the radio. The Chris Evans breakfast show would do until 'Pop Master' with the jovial Jock, Ken Bruce came on at ten-thirty. Gethin was determined to call in and play the game sometime soon. He fancied strutting around the park in a 'One Year Out' T-shirt.

***

The Grey Mercedes pulled to the kerb and the driver stepped out. A light rain spat droplets onto the highly waxed paintwork. The car was less than a month old, a present from his bestie. He knew he was lucky. He knew his best pal thought so too. The luck could run out soon but pushing the limits was all part and parcel of the fun. It added the edge to his game and life wasn't worth living without the edge.

He walked to the rear and removed a small rucksack from the back seat. Locking the car, he slipped his arms into the straps and began a fast jog from the main road and up along the concrete entry road leading to Trecco Bay caravan park.

He kept a steady pace until he reached the caravan. The van was a clone of the others on either side of it; white, long, shiny and convenient. He jiggled the key into the lock and stepped inside the L-shaped kitchen. A small digital radio was the only object visible on the worktops. He liked to keep the van clean and clear of clutter. He selected Radio Two and heard the infectious laughter of Chris Evans the presenter. He checked his watch, just in time to hear the day's 'show-stopper' tunes. Rainbow began blasting their one and only monster hit as he slipped out of his tracksuit and underwear.

He stood in the full length mirror attached to the wall next to the door and admired his nakedness. Satisfied, he pulled a flesh-like mask from the kit bag and pulled it over his head. From a distance it looked real. Leonard DiCaprio would have a coronary if he knew.

The man slipped his feet back into his trainers and checked the coast was clear. He knew the caravans on either side of him were empty. The owners to the left were a pharmacist and his wife who rarely seemed to have time to use their holiday home, whilst the van to the right was owned by a retired couple. They wouldn't come back to the park for another week or so and by that time his game would go onto hold.

**

The dry air from the central heating system was making Janice sleepy. If she didn't move she'd be flat out soon.

"Fancy a cuppa, Geth'?"

Gethin stretched and yawned. The week had been chaotic in the pharmacy. Another year and that would be it. He couldn't do it any longer. He had to retire. There'd be more time to spend in the caravan and he'd promised Babs that he'd take her to Mauritius.

"Aye, a coffee would be nice," he said.

Janice walked four steps from the lounge to the kitchen and took the kettle off the heating stand and filled it under the tap. She yawned again as the water began to rise. The weather wasn't ideal for an overnight stay. She looked out the kitchen window at the sky and noticed the door to the caravan next door begin to open. That was strange. She didn't think they would be there at this time of the year. The door opened fully and she froze. Leonardo DiCaprio was standing in the doorway of the next-door caravan in Trecco Bay, totally bollock naked.

ANOTHER TWO BODIES

No sooner had I tasked Churchy and Jane than Jeff rushed into the office. "Boss, you are not going to believe this...two more youngsters have been found dead in Pencoed.

I felt that dread in my stomach again.

"Both found by a dog walker on the Woodland Avenue playing fields," Jeff continued. "Apparently, his dog started sniffing around the large metal rugby equipment container. The door was ajar and when he looked inside, there they were, laid out on the tackle bags."

"Who's at the scene, Jeff?"

"Everybody, boss. The world and his fucking wife. The Super, the whole shooting match."

That wasn't good news. "Give Steve a shout for me, Jeff. I'll get straight down there and meet him."

This was now getting totally out of hand.

We arrived at the playing fields and, to be fair to the local lads, the whole area had been cordoned off. A young PC, holding a clipboard was checking everybody in and out.

We showed him our ID's and signed his sheet. I whispered in his ear, "No press okay? Any problems, you give me shout."

"No problem, sir, I've already been briefed."

Many times in the past, I've attended scenes of serious crime to find all fucking sorts mooching around. The worse are senior officers who just want to have a look and be seen to be doing something. The motorway police patrols call the public who do this sort of thing at accident, 'rubber neckers.' The press just as bad, so cunning, do anything for a good shot. Mind you, any reporter worth his salt would be all over this like a rash. I accepted the press motives, even if I didn't always like them. I couldn't accept incompetence from senior officers. They should know better.

We made our way to the container. The gang was all there, Hugo, Glyn the SOCO, DC Peter Harding, the Duty Inspector and Sergeant, oh aye, and the knob-head Super.

I was relieved to see the Inspector and Sergeant, bearing in mind what had happened up in Maesteg on Monday. Seemed like there was a bit more shape on this pair.

Both bodies were inside the container, an old rusty shipping container the club had probably acquired from some 'friend of the club.' The dead boys were flat out on tackle bags, both with the needles in their arms, and all the works alongside.

What a way to die, amongst dirty old rugby kit and tackle machines. I felt really miserable, but I had to get to the bottom of this and the quicker the better.

"Any ID on the pair of them?" I asked.

"Nothing, boss," Pete Harding replied, "just a couple of mobile phones, some lighters, cigarettes and a small plastic bag with some powder inside."

"Check the phone companies; see if you can access contacts. Any missing persons reported?"

"No, boss, none at all."

"They've got to be local," I said. "It won't be long before someone misses them."

I had a chat with Hugo and Glyn, it was the same scenario as young Pye and Leanne Morgan – or whatever the hell her name was.

I felt my phone vibrating in my jacket pocket. I pulled it out and looked at the 'call listing.' It was the lab.'

"The powder from Pye and the mystery woman was exactly same," the metallic voice announced with certainty. "Ninety percent pure heroin, cut with a little baking powder."

I told them that I was at the scene of what appeared to be a double drug fatality, and that similar powder had been recovered.

"As long as you get it to us before close of play we'll give it priority and you could probably have the result in the morning."

That was impressive. I left the rest to Glyn, he knew the score and how important the analysis would be.

I then had a chat with the Super' – thought I better had. "I'll organise some house to house in the vicinity," he said.

Not such a bell-end after all.

I nodded in agreement, someone had to do it. "These two young lads probably made their way to the container under the cover of darkness."

The Super' seemed to agree.

Steve and I then left the scene and made our way back to the office.

En route, I phoned Jeff to get the whole team back in the office as soon as possible and within the hour the whole team was assembled.

"Thank you, ladies and gentlemen, I've got you all together to bring you up to speed with regard to the recent drug related deaths. It would appear that there is a bad batch of heroin doing the rounds in the division, not that any of the shit is good, but you know what I mean. I believe it's been instrumental in the death of Alan Pye at Maesteg and a woman who we first thought was Leanne Morgan in Bridgend. It now looks like she might not be Leanne but some Polish woman. We now also have the two unknown males in Pencoed.

"The lab has confirmed that the heroin recovered in Maesteg and Bridgend is from the same batch and I have no doubt the Pencoed one will be the same.

"We've recovered three mobile phones from the deceased and Tech' Support will be doing the business on them for us.

They're giving it priority to see if there's any connection between these youngsters and a possible supplier, but then again, you know how cunning these fucking suppliers are.

"Steve and Col'? I want you to split the teams up, I want men out on the ground in Bridgend, Maesteg, Porthcawl and Pencoed this evening until about eleven.

"Speak to your narks, let's see if we can find out what twat is supplying this shit to our kids.

"Churchy, Jane, before you go. Any update on the woman previously known as Leanne Morgan?"

Jane flipped open her notes. "Leanne had been working at Zircon for about two months. All documentation they held was in that name, as far as they were concerned she was just with them through an agency. That all checks out as legit' as well.

"To be fair, boss, we had the impression they didn't much care where she was from only that she did her job.

"As for the name, Rosanna Balcoff? SB is following that up with the Immigration."

"Any theories about Leanne? Let me know what you're thinking," I said.

Jane looked at Churchy, who nodded. "I think she's been trafficked boss," Jane added. "I also think that the landlord, this bloke called Brean, is not telling the truth. It's just intuition an,d excuse my French, but I think he was shagging her."

"Fair enough," I said. "That's a good shout. Leave Mr Brean to me. Okay everybody, Izzy, fucking wizzy, let's get fucking busy! Knock-off about eleven. Don't come back to the office, go straight home and rest. See you back here at eight am sharp."

Mike and I didn't go home, we thought if the troops were out late, it wouldn't be fair. I knew it would upset Molly, especially with Chris at home too, but what could I do?

I had plenty to occupy my mind, trying to piece it all together.

I had a call from DC Peter Harding, just a little after nine.

"Hello, boss. We've identified the two young lads and, wait for it…they're brothers. Paul and Scott Hatton, seventeen and nineteen years of age. Both live with their parents on the local council estate. Both known to the local bobbies, but no previous. The parents have been informed, I did that myself and also had a good look in their rooms…"

"And?"

"Nothing found, boss, looks like their Mam is a prolific cleaner, everything in its place. Their parents are heartbroken. I've also done the formal ID at the morgue; I believe the PM is in the morning."

"If you hear anything of any value, give me ring," I said as I ended the call.

Mike sat quietly, he could tell by my expression that the call wasn't delivering good news.

"So that's it, Mike, four dead in four days. What a dreadful way for young kids to die. It's the fucking scourge of the country and I promise we're going to lock up the fucker responsible for a very long time. "

I kept thinking about my two kids and what it would be like if me and Molly ever lost one of them. I honestly don't know what we would do. To lose one must be horrendous, but to lose two at the same time must be the most devastating thing that could happen to anyone?

When this was all over, I'd make a point of visiting the Hatton's, hopefully with some form of good news?

THE CARVAN

A young man stood behind the reception desk, tall, lean, barely able to sprout his first facial growth, yet determined beyond his age and experience.

"I'm sorry, I can't give you that information," he said for the third time of asking.

Caroline sighed. This wasn't going to be easy. "Look, it doesn't have to be like this. All I'm asking for is the name of the owner of caravan..." she checked her notes, "...F29. It's not rocket science and it's not going to get you into trouble."

He shook his head and folded his arms, a defensive gesture, a physical punctuation to the conversation. As far as he was concerned, this was the end of the conversation.

Caroline had run out of patience. "Let me speak to your manager."

"Not here," he snapped. "Told you that already."

The office was empty, that was a blessing. Caroline knew what she had to do and she didn't want anyone else to be a witness to it. "Listen to me, you little jumped-up shit. I've been working on this case for far too long. This is my first real break. This information could help me catch this pervert who happens to be running around the park flashing his bits to anyone and everyone. If you don't give me the name and address of the owner right this minute I'm going to arrest you for obstruction. 'll get a warrant and have a police van and a dozen hairy-arsed coppers down here in double-quick time. Imagine the embarrassment. Do you know what your manager will say when that happens?"

The first crack. The young lad's resolve was breaking. "You can't do that. We haven't done anything wrong. I'm not trying to be awkward. We value our customers' privacy..."

"That's right. You haven't done anything wrong and I understand the need to keep the customers sweet. I'm guessing that the manager would love to help us, too. He doesn't want a fucking idiot running naked around the park, does he?"

"Of course not."

"What do you think he'd do if he was here now?"

"I dunno," the lad said.

"I do," Caroline snapped firmly. "He'd take the records off the computer and hand them over to me in the best interests of the business and all the good people of this park. Now, be a good lad and get the owner details for me before I step around there and show you the error of your ways."

His face flushed. "Okay," he said. "But I'll tell my manager that you forced me. I'll make a complaint..."

Caroline held up her hand. "Stop!" she shouted. "I don't care what you say or do. I just want the name."

The receptionist sat at his computer terminal and trawled through a screen of data. "Here," he said. "You better write it down. I'm not printing it. All prints are logged on the system."

Lifting the counter hatch, Caroline stepped over to the computer as the young lad slid his seat out of strike range.

"Thank you," she said as she looked at the name in the log. She read the name and address twice then gripped the edge of the table. "Ohhhh...myyyy...God," she said slowly as the data finally registered.

BREAN INTERVIEW

The squad were all in, bright eyed and bushy tailed. I just hoped they'd gleaned some information and intelligence on the identity of the supplier?

Unfortunately, it wasn't to be. We were no further on in identifying the bastard who was responsible for killing these kids.

One thing that did come out of the exercise was that after speaking to the narks, we discovered that, apparently, there was a short supply of heroin in the area. Most users were doing coke and speed.

I was also aware that, geographically, all the deaths were more or less in a straight line, Pencoed, Bridgend and Maesteg, nothing to the West and nothing to the East of the division.

This got me thinking. Is there a new supplier on the scene, are the dead individuals connected in any way? I had no idea.

I made the decision there and then to concentrate the squad in those areas. I wanted them to put pressure on known drug suppliers, turn their houses over, stop and search them, make their lives a misery.

I gave them a free rein; hopefully, by doing this, we might get the answer we desperately needed.

In the meantime, the lab confirmed that the heroin responsible for all the deaths was from the same batch.

I just hoped that the fucking supplier had run out of his stash. The next few days would be critical and I prayed there'd be no more deaths.

About midday, I received a call from DS Aled POWELL down at the airport SB office.

"Boss, looks like Immigration has identified the young woman for you. Her name is Rosanna Balcoff. Born 11.8.1994 in Warsaw, Poland. Not known to the Police or Immigration.

I'll wire her passport details and photograph to you directly. What do you make of it all, boss?"

I thanked him. "To be honest," I said. "It's a bit puzzling. One of my DC's thinks she's been trafficked, but that's just a theory."

I was expecting some sort of negation from the other end of the line but didn't get it. "Well, boss, trafficking is definitely on the up. The Immigration boys have noticed a dramatic increase during this last twelve months. It's big money now."

"I was afraid you were going to say that."

"If there's anything else we can do, just give me a bell, all the best," he said and hung up.

Within a few minutes, Rosanna's photograph, together with all her passport details, was on my desk. The definition and detail of the image was second to none, not like years ago when you could hardly make a nose out on a face.

I had Jeff to contact Churchy and Jane to call back to the office and, hopefully, confirm the Identification.

The more I thought about it, the more sense it made. What if Rosanna had arrived in this country and had been propositioned by some scumbag, who had put her to work, or even pimped her out?

Perhaps Horace Brean, could throw a little light on it?

***

Churchy and Jane were back within the hour, they took one look at the photo and without blinking an eye confirmed that the dead girl was, in fact, Rosanna Balcoff.

My phone rang and the voice of the ACC wasn't something I particularly wanted to hear at that moment.

"Hello, Terry. I know you're up to your eyes with the drug deaths, but just to let you know, I've fixed a conference at HQ for twelve-midday on Monday. All representatives will be there to plan the way forward in relation to Hydra. You okay with that?"

No problem, boss. I'll bring Mike and Steve my DS, and a couple of DC's along with me. See you Monday."

I put the phone down. I sighed. It never rains but it always seems to fucking pour. One thing about it, we would still have an important role to play in what I could see being a major international drug smuggling sting.

I had a bit of lunch with Mike - another bag of bloody chips - and then made my way to "Bryntirion," the home of Horace BREAN.

On my way, I was thinking, about how I should play it with him. Go in heavy, straight off the bat, or be empathetic with him?

I had already looked into his background; the man was a fucking pervert - end of. That could well be the weakness I could exploit.

I pulled up outside the house and walked up the drive towards the front door. I could see a man who answered the description of Brean in the window. This bloke obviously didn't miss much.

Before I I had the chance to knock, Brean opened the door.

"I'm Detective Chief Inspector Terry McGuire and I'm investigating the death of Rosanna, one of your lodgers."

"Rosanna? Who the hell is that?"

I sighed. I didn't want to play games. I needed to get to the bottom of this, fast. "Look, Mr Brean. We've discovered that the woman we thought was Leanne Morgan is in fact Rossana Balcoff."

I could tell by his expression that this wasn't news to Brean.

"Oh, my God. Come on in, Chief, how can I help you?"

We made our way into the front room and I sat on a dining room chair. I didn't fancy the sofa or easy chairs, they had seen better days, the place was like a shit house and I had no way of knowing what kinds of liquids or solids had found their way onto the dark brown Dralon covers.

"Cup of tea, Chief?"

"No thank you, Horace, and please, call me Terry and I'll cut to the chase."

Brean looked disappointed. Perhaps he didn't get many social calls? Then again, going by the state of his settee, I wasn't surprised.

"When did you first meet Rosanna?"

I met LEANNE..." he said, emphasising that he had no idea that her real name was Rossana. Fucking liar. "...about three month ago. I advertise in the Glamorgan Gazette that I've got rooms-to-let and she turned up with her case."

"Was she alone or was she with anyone?"

"Alone, I believe."

I didn't believe it, not for a moment.

"You believe, Horace? Either she was, or she fucking wasn't? Now shape up."

"There's no need to talk like that, Terry," he retorted.

"Listen now, Horace and fucking listen good because I'm only going to say this once. I'm investigating the deaths of four youngsters, including Rosanna, and I believe you hold the fucking key. Now, you answer my questions or I'll be arresting you in connection with these deaths."

I saw Brean's bottom lip start to quiver and his body language changed, I'd hit a nerve.

"Now let's start again, Horace. Was there anybody with her when she came here first?"

He looked at the floor, and said, "I daren't tell you anything, Terry. I'm sorry, but I can't."

Horace, you've got a bit of form for Indecency and you're in your fifties, a ten-stretch isn't going to do you any good, and look, you're like a tub of fucking lard. Lots of blokes inside the nick love little round men. I'm sure they'll love you there. You'd better start co-operating or I'll lock you up, I fucking guarantee it."

He cupped his head in his hands and mumbled, "What do you want to know?"

"I want to know exactly what's been going on in relation to Rosanna and any other girls that you've rented rooms to?"

Brean mumbled, "They'll do me if they know I've been talking to you."

"That's your choice, Horace. Talk to me now or it's down to the nick, it's fucking up to you."

Brean composed himself, took a deep breath then exhaled slowly. I could smell the stale tobacco on his breath. "Ask your questions, you're a bit of bastard, aren't you?"

"I certainly am, Horace, I have to be, especially when kids are dropping like flies having jacked up on pure fucking poison. Tell me about Rosanna, how she got here and who brought her?"

He leaned against the wall. "Like I said, she turned up about three months ago?"

Don't tell me what I already know," I warned him. "Who was with her?"

"A Polish bloke, in a white Transit van."

"Any names?"

"No, just turned up with Rosanna and enquired about a room. I had one spare, he paid the fifty-quid rent and he left her. Rosanna then paid the rent herself every Friday after that.

"What sort of girl was Rosanna, was she Polish as well?"

"Yes. Her English was fairly good, but she was pretty and very polite. I liked her."

"Was she the first girl that this guy brought here?"

Brean dropped his head and mumbled, "No."

"So there have been more, Horace?"

"Yes, three others over the last year and the same bloke brought them. They only stay for a couple of months then they're off again."

"So you're telling me that over the last twelve months, you have put up four young women at the behest of this bloke?"

He looked very sheepish. "Yes, I thought nothing of it; I didn't ask questions, it's none of my business. You know what these Poles are like, they keep themselves to themselves."

"Have you got the names of the other girls, Horace? This is very important, they could be in danger or even dead?"

"Listen, Terry, I'm not involved in any drug shit, honestly, all I've done is rent the room."

"I believe you, Horace, many fucking wouldn't. But listen now, you're not a dull bloke, if anything, I would say you're pretty fucking shrewd, you don't miss a trick sitting by your front window watching the world go by. I believe you have a little Insurance, knowing the day of reckoning would come, am I right?"

"I don't know what you mean, Terry," he blustered.

"Horace, don't fuck me about. You've been good as gold so far, now tell me, where's the Insurance?"

Brean stepped from the wall and paced around for a moment. He kept biting his fist and I could see his mind was in turmoil. Finally, he nodded his head and walked into the living room. I followed him and saw him pick up a biscuit tin from the floor next to his chair. "It's in here, vehicle numbers, the names of all my lodgers and the rent amounts."

Brean gave me the book and I flicked through it, everything was there - dates, vehicles, names and amounts.

"Cheers, Horace. I'll get one of my boys to go through this down at the office later."

His face drained of colour. "Oh fuck, you aren't going to arrest me are you, Terry?"

"No, Horace, you can be our star witness when we bring this fucking lot to book."

"They'll kill me," he pleaded.

"Horace, in this game, it's look after number one. You dance with the devil and you get your arse burnt. Is there anything else you want to tell me?"

"No, that's all of it."

"Do you remember Jane, my DC who came here initially?"

"Yes, pretty girl, why?"

"Well, she tells me that you were obviously upset when she told you Rosanna was dead, were you having a relationship with her?"

Brean then shocked me. He broke down and started crying, "Fuck no," he sobbed. "I liked her and spent some time in her room, just talking, she was a sad young woman. I knew she was on drugs, but I didn't have any of the old feelings for her, I swear. To be honest with you, I haven't been with a woman for many years, I'm fucked in that department, Terry, can't even raise a smile anymore. Took drugs off a friend who said it would stop it...you know...those feelings."

"And it worked?"

"Nearly killed me. Fucked my prostate and now I'm no danger to anyone."

Shit! Wasn't expecting that lot.

"Okay, Horace, this is the plan. I take you down the office, have one of the lads to take a full statement off you and go through the book with him, you okay with that? The most important thing is the van registration and the names of the girls."

Brean began to panic and grabbed my arm. "You're not arresting me are you, Terry? Promise!"

"No, Horace I already promised. You're a witness, that's all."

MANY HEADS OF HYDRA

I sat with my specially selected team of officers amongst a dour bunch of jumped-up twats from the other agencies tasked with sorting out Hydra.

Colin, my DS, and three good DC's, Bryn Thomas, Tom Powell and Stan Gibbs were looking smug, knowing they were about to get a prolonged attachment to the Sussex Constabulary to tie up the loose ends of Hydra. Hydra had escalated from a local drugs bust into a multi-agency operation that we had to hand over.

Detective Superintendent Briers from the Sussex force sat behind a large oak desk in a room our force used to coordinate major incidents, rather originally named the 'Major Incident Room.' Briers had a long, thin face that gave him the appearance of the ex-football league manager Jimmy Hill. The only thing missing was the silly bit of hair on the end of his pointy chin. He obviously liked to look important, his suit was expensive, charcoal grey with a pointlessly thin pinstripe that could hardly be noticed. This bloke liked to spend his dosh on his clothes.

Alongside the Super was one of the bigwigs from Customs, a guy called David Kinnock. He too was immaculately dressed in a dark-blue blazer and grey trousers. He sat with his legs crossed so tightly I couldn't help wondering if he had any bollocks between his legs?

Kinnock was tall and lean and completely bald but his face showed signs of a penchant for a tipple or two. Tiny red and blue thread veins littered his cheeks and his complexion looked anything but healthy.

Our ACC, Alan Chambers chaired the meeting. He sat in a high-back leather chair alongside Briers and, to me, I thought he looked a little lost, like a schoolboy recently berated for being naughty in class.

The ACC spoke. "Thank you all for joining me today. I asked Detective

Superintendent Briers to come her to get a briefing on Hydra. As you all know by now, Hydra has become a multi-agency operation. As the central focus for the investigation seems to be in Sussex, we will now be running this under the command of Mr Briers. Mr Kinnock here will co-ordinate the Customs end of things."

Kinnock nodded and seemed to be glowering at me.

"I'll kick things off by asking Detective Chief Inspector McGuire to fill us in on the scores-on-the-door," the ACC added.

I looked at the two heads of the team and coughed to clear my throat. "I believe you all have the files my team compiled with all the information you need?"

Briers and Kinnock nodded.

"Then there's no point in going through it all again. We've got a pressing matter involving several drug deaths in out force area and unless there are any questions, I'd like to suggest that we knock this on the head now. My DS and DC's here are happy to act as liaisons with Sussex and the Customs and will help in any operational matter at your end. If that's all?"

Kinnock's face seemed to turn a brighter shade of red. "Can you tell me why we weren't involved at an earlier stage in the investigation?"

I wanted to say something about not trusting the bastards to not fuck it up but thought better of it. "I'm sorry, sir, but we had something we felt had limited interest to Customs. The information was gathered through our SB at the airport and nothing was actually brought through Customs there. It quickly became apparent that the importation was being focussed elsewhere, outside of our area, and it was then we decided to pass it on."

"You still went to Calais without informing us," he fumed.

"Operational necessity. Shit happens," I said.

The ACC chipped in. He knew me only too well and picked up on my rising anger. "I think what's happened has happened. I'm afraid we can't change that. At least now we have something we can work on together."

I caught sight of a brief grin from Briers but I wasn't sure if it was a good or bad type.

Kinnock clearly wanted to get his dig in. "I'm not sure if it's wise to involve South Wales Police in this. We need a team that will be open and share intelligence..."

I stood up and stopped the twat in his tracks. "Just hold on a minute, butt," I said. I looked toward Briers and could see that grin again. "We've handed you a cracker of a job, on a plate. How many times have you lot withheld stuff from us?"

"So you did deliberately withhold it from us?" Kinnock growled.

"What's more important here, the fact that a major international drug operation could soon be blown out of the water or the fact that your fucking pride has been hurt?"

Kinnock looked flustered. I don't think anyone could have ever stood up to him before. Briers grin got wider. But the ACC was clearly embarrassed. "Okay, okay," the ACC said. "That's all, Terry. Please sit down."

Kinnock looked quickly between the ACC and Briers but Briers was openly chuckling to himself. Kinnock quickly realised that he wasn't going to get the support he expected from Briers and the ACC.

Briers held up his hand as I sat back in my chair. I could hear Colin and my DC's sniggering alongside me and I must admit I felt guilty letting them see me act in that way but I've always had a low threshold of tolerance for twats.

"I'm happy to take your team back with me to Sussex," Briers said. "I've heard quite a bit about the team and I have to say I'm impressed with the way you've pulled together over the last few weeks, especially after the incident with the previous D.C.I."

I looked at Colin with raised eyebrows. The bloke had done his research, or the ACC had filled him in?

He then ran through the expectations and aspirations of the Sussex force and I excused myself to get back to the real work at hand. I knew Colin and the others would make me proud.

***

I made it home briefly for some lunch. I felt guilty as it wasn't often I got to see my son.

I called in the Tesco petrol station on the way and bought a bunch of flowers for Molly and, even though they weren't particularly expensive, I thought they looked pretty.

I walked into the house and found Molly and Chris dressed up and looking like they were about to go out.

"Oh, those are lovely, Terry," she said, as I handed her the bouquet.

She passed them over to Chris, "Fetch a vase from the cupboard in the corner," she said. Chris obliged.

"Off out?" I asked.

She smiled. "Chris is taking me to The Vale of Glamorgan for a meal. Are you going to come with us?"

"I can't," I said and could see the smile slip from Molly's face.

"No. Don't suppose you can," she added icily.

"You know what it's like, Mol,'" I said.

"Only too well, Terry."

"Look, let's not do this just now, eh?" I said.

"Your son has come home to visit and you've not spent any time with him. He goes back to Hong Kong in a couple of days."

"I know, Molly. I'm sorry," I turned to Chris for moral support but I can see he's avoiding eye contact with me. Can't blame him.

"I'll get things tied up and spend some time with you before you go back," I said to Chris.

He forced a smile as he filled the vase with water. "No problem, dad. Don't worry."

I heard the sound of a car horn.

"That's the taxi, mam," Chris said. He took some coats from the cupboard under the stairs and helped my wife out of the house.

The door closed behind them and I stood there for God knows how long, just looking at the door and wondering how the hell I got myself into this position?

STEVE DIAMOND INFORMATION

After getting the relevant information out of Horace, I hooked him down to the office.

I introduced the slime-bag to Jeff and I then tasked my office manager with the taking of a detailed statement relating to the goings on at "Bryntirion" over the last twelve months. I wanted to know everything.

Jeff was eager to help, he'd been out of the game for a few weeks and I could see the delight in his face, now he was involved in something he must have felt was more important than managing the day-to-day tedious stuff. Truth was, Jeff was doing a cracking job for me and I couldn't think of anyone who could have done it better.

He led Horace off into the Interview room, "Bleed the fucker dry, Jeff," I called after him.

Horace looked back over his shoulder at me, "You're a hard bastard, fair play Terry, a hard bastard."

I laughed, poured myself a coffee and started trying to clear my desk of all the bureaucratic crap that came across it on a daily basis.

I hadn't even had a sip of coffee, nor moved a sheet of paper when the phone rang.

"McGuire, who's speaking?"

"It's me Ter,' Steve, Steve Diamond."

I was shocked to hear from Steve again so soon. He had been locked up for murder and began serving his sentence down in Dartmoor. During the investigation into the corrupt coppers, Steve's name had come up and I'd paid him a visit at prison. His information had certainly made the convictions a lot easier and I had made a promise that I'd try and get him moved closer to home. He had got the move but no thanks to me. I had intended keeping my promise to him but it seems someone else had done the good deed before me and Steve Diamond thought it was down to me. He now thought my shit was chocolate.

"What the fuck do you want now, Steve, nobody hanging is there?" I couldn't help but laugh because one of the bent coppers had taken his own life in his cell. I could hear Steve snigger too.

"The twat had it coming, Ter,' you know that, butt. Anyway, fuck Ambrose, he's history."

I couldn't agree more.

"I may have got something for you? It's going back a few years, a murder in Maesteg around the mid-nineties. I think you call them 'cold cases' these days, ironic really, I was thinking about Reggie Hughes."

Reggie had been found on a beach in Porthcawl and had been stuffed in a chest freezer in Ambrose's house for five years prior to the bent twat trying to flush him out to sea.

"Go on, Steve, you have my ear."

"Just the one, Ter?'" he tittered.

"Since it's you, Steve, I'll lend you both, butt."

"Well, a couple of days ago, I shared a cell with a bloke from Garw, a bloke called Gerry Murphey. He was only an overnighter, being moved on the following morning. Anyway, we get chatting, like you do, and your name crops up. Fuck me, I thought, Terry's a busy little bee. He said you did him for burglary, going back a few years ago, but thinks you're a tidy bloke. I put him right on that, of course," he laughed.

"Get to the fucking point, Steve. I'm drowning in dead bodies here at the moment, butt."

Steve cleared his throat and I could hear him mumble something.

"What's that?" I asked.

"Not talking to you, Ter,' got a bit of a queue forming for the fucking phone, like. You know what it's like, butt."

"Thankfully, I don't, Steve," I corrected him, and I hoped I would remain unfamiliar with the social niceties of prison life.

"Well," Steve continued, "he says he knows who did the murder. Says the bloke has no form and wasn't even interviewed about it. He didn't elaborate, only said that the fella used a hammer on a dealer from Pontycymer."

I made the connection. What Steve said certainly began ringing bells."

"I think he's after a few bob, Ter,' to be honest, but you never know, do you?"

"Where's he been shipped out to, Steve?"

Steve laughed. "Funny thing is, he's now on the Moor, that's fucking ironic as well, Ter,' what you reckon?"

"Will he talk to me?"

"I think so, he gave me that impression."

"Thank you, Steve, leave it with me. I may as well have fucking digs up on the Moor, the time I've spent down there of late."

"Aye, that's what I was thinking."

"Anyway, how's the family?"

"Fucking brilliant, Ter,' fair play, see them regular, thanks to you..."

I could hear another kerfuffle on the other end of the line.

"You alright there, Steve?"

"Aye, I'm alright. Got to go now, there's a six-foot fucking Adonis waiting to use the phone, he's looking nasty, so I better fuck off."

Fuck me, I thought, a cold case on top of everything? I just hoped it wasn't a load of old bollocks.

I remembered the murder as if it was yesterday. I was a DS on Division at the time. The victim was a second-hand dealer and drug supplier from Pontycymer.

His body was found up in the Maesteg Forestry and his van at the bottom of Bettws Hill.

It was like three murders in one, a real shit job of an enquiry.

I wasn't directly involved in the enquiry, but I knew it had never been detected, and I knew for a fact it had been reviewed a few times since, with no luck.

I decided to put it on the back-burner for the moment because I wanted to protect the living. The dead could wait just a little longer.

Now all I could do was wait for Jeff to top and tail Horace and hopefully start locking up some bad-arsed drug suppliers.

OBSERVATIONS

After taking the statement off Brean, arrangements were made for him to be returned home. I had a quick chat to him and told him we would look after him, the usual sort of shit – a regular uniform drive by, immediate response to his calls, etc, personally, I didn't really give a fuck about him, but then again he was our star witness, and we needed him. This was a case of pulling out all the stops to protect someone who really didn't deserve protecting. I'd rather have been straight with him and told him to go and scratch my arse, but there was more at stake here.

Jeff had informed me that he had found four female names in the book and only one van registration Number.

"Don't tell me, Jeff, re-call the squad. I think it's time for a conference, and guess what?"

"What boss?"

"You can give the briefing," I smirked.

"But don't you want to know now?" he protested.

"No, Jeff, this one is yours, butt."

Within half an hour the squad were all assembled.

"Ladies and Gents," I began, "this is where we are at the moment in relation to the drug deaths.

"I believe that the death of Rosanna Balcoff is tied to the deaths of Alan Pye and the two Hatton brothers. The same batch of heroin killed them all.

"I also believe that Rosanna has been trafficked together with other young Polish women.

"Jeff has obtained a full detailed statement off that fat slimy bastard, Horace Brean and I have no doubt that Jeff holds the key to the whole enquiry." I looked at Jeff and I could see him take a deep breath, his chest inflated and I think he finally understood how important he was to me and the team. "Over to you, Jeff," I announced.

There was a big cheer from the team and some whistles as Jeff took to the floor, he was bombarded with paper planes and polystyrene coffee cups. Fair play to him, he took it all in good part and ducked and dived better than Mohammed Ali.

"That's enough boys and girls," I said. "What have we got, Jeff?"

"Right, boss, the description of the Polish bloke, the twat responsible for dropping these girls off at Brean's, is as follows…he's approximately, six-foot tall, black curly hair, full black beard like one of those fashionable twats…"

Someone interrupted, "I think it's called a Hipster?"

Jeff shrugged. "Okay, he's looks like a Hipster twat." The team laughed again. "Aged about 40, the only name he gave Brean was 'Jar,' as in glass pot used to hold jam or to piss in."

"No fucking missing him then, boys and girls?" I said.

Jeff continued, "The van he was driving is a white Ford Transit, registration number Charlie-Kilo-zero-five November-November-Zulu, registered to "CARVAL," Bridgend Road, Maesteg.

"Three other young girls, apart from Rosanna, have lived at Brean's, but only for a few months at a time. This bloke, Jar moves them on, but their names are listed as; Suzanne Ryan, Michelle Davies, Roxanne Smyth, also probably false names."

"What do you reckon then, Jeff?" I asked.

He thought for a brief moment and another comedian in my group shouted, "I can hear the cogs moving, boss." I grinned. The banter was part and parcel of the job. Every copper had to learn to take it early on or they wouldn't last long.

"Well, after interviewing Brean," Jeff said, "and then hearing about all the circumstances surrounding Rosanna, I would say that they're definitely being trafficked, and god knows where they are now, they could all be dead as far as we know?"

"Well, you've all heard what Jeff thinks, any ideas?" I threw the question out to the team.

One of the DC's, Alan Smith, raised his hand, "I know the premises, boss, run by a few Poles, car wash, car valeting, the usual, you know what they're like, working like dogs almost twenty-four-seven."

"Could we get an OP on it Al,' tonight up until about midday tomorrow?"

"Should be no problem, boss," he nodded. "It's the old Opal garage, with a forecourt where the petrol pumps used to be. They're using the main office. Leave it to me. I'll take the obs' van up and do an overnighter."

"Any other volunteers?"

DC Keith Woodley raised his hand. "I'll do it with him, boss. I'm used to his smells."

"Pot and kettle comes to mind," Alan replied, smiling.

"Excellent, boys. The van and this fucker called Jar are the priority," I said. "The squad will be on standby from about eight in the morning and if both are there, we'll call a strike. I want this bastard so bad it's giving me palpitations.

"Alan and Keith? You crack on. Give me a ring when you're plotted up and if there are any sightings worth reporting."

"Will do, boss, we'll be on plot by about six-ish and we'll give you a bell."

I smiled warmly. This team had shaped up and I was proud of the way they had responded to me over the past few weeks. "Okay everybody, get home, rest up. I've got a good feeling about this one. Before you go, operational name please, Jeff?"

He didn't have to think. He must have been pondering this from the outset. "Operation 'GDANSK,' boss."

"Fuck me Jeff," I laughed. "How original."

THE STRIKE AND ARREST

Alan and Keith had plotted up on time and reported back that it was all pretty quiet at the car wash.

There was no sign of the Transit or Jar, there were only four workers on the forecourt and they appeared youngsters - aged between about twenty and twenty-five.

I had all the team on standby for the call from Alan and Keith. All the vehicles were gassed-up and now all we could do was wait.

This could turn out to be a long shift for Alan and Keith, but I reckoned it would be well worth it, the old gut feeling.

I was back in the office at seven, together with Mike, Steve and Colin, and we discussed the strategy regarding a possible strike.

The cars and bike would plot up near to the car wash if Jar and the Transit turned up.

Keith and Smithy would give the heads up, and one of the cars would pull on to the forecourt as a prospective customer, but only when Jar was in the office and alone.

As soon as this opportunity arose, Smithy and Keith would call the strike and Jar would be taken down and arrested.

By eight, all the squad had turned up and were properly briefed by Steve and Mike, I could see they were eager to get going, they were on a roll.

As the morning progressed, there was still no sighting of the Transit or Jar, just the four young car washers going about their business.

I then decided to send the squad up the valley, to be nearer to the premises.

Mike, Jeff and I remained in the office, listening to the infrequent communications between the members of the team. I just hoped the next voice we would hear would be Keith or Smithy.

We only had to wait about an hour, I could hear Smithy bellowing, *"Target and vehicle approaching forecourt from the direction of Bridgend, repeat, target and vehicle approaching forecourt!"*

These are the moments we live for, the adrenalin pumps and the hair rises on the back of the head.

"Vehicle now on forecourt and parked near office," Smithy called in.

"Target out of vehicle and entering office, joining two of the young car washers…"

"Target, waving arms and gesturing young men to leave the office, he's following them, looks like he's in a real rip and tamping with them…"

"Three vehicle being washed, now all four youngsters busy…"

"Target standing outside office, waving arms and shouting..."

"Target now back in office alone and has pulled the door shut..."

"Strike, strike, strike!"

***

Steve and Colin raced on to the forecourt and rushed from their car. They burst through the office door and tackled an angry looking Jar. Jar struggled but was overpowered and cuffed.

The rest of the squad were there in a moment, like rats up drainpipes. They were out of their vehicles and corralling the four youngsters by the office door.

Jane had parked her bike and was now informing all the civvies to move their vehicles - the car wash was now closed for business for the foreseeable future.

Steve formally arrested Jar on suspicion of people trafficking and supplying Class A drugs.

By this time Smithy and Keith had made their way to the office and, together with Colin, made a search of the office.

The office was quite sparse and Jar wasn't very forthcoming when spoken to, what we like to term, 'keeping mum.'

Colin then pulled back a piece of floor-lino and found a hatch which opened up on to a floor safe.

"Where's the key?" Steve snarled.

"Fuck you!" Jar growled.

Steve pushed Jar against a wall and checked through his pockets. The stupid fucker had the safe key in his pocket with a plastic tag attached labelled with the words 'Safe Key.'

Steve opened the safe. It was like Pandora's Box, nine Polish passports, ten-grand in cash and about half a kilo of white powder.

Steve called a DC in to bag and tag the goodies.

Jar knew there was no point in continuing to struggle. They were all outnumbered and none of my team was in the mood to mess about. Jar and the four youngsters were roughly bundled across the yard and stuffed into the police cars and conveyed to Bridgend Bridewell.

Myself and Mike followed and conferred with them all there.

I had already given the heads up to the Custody Sergeant, Malcolm Old. I told him about the Op' and to expect a few prisoners. I'd known Mal' for most of my service. Mal' was old school, liked a pint or two, but was sound, and I knew he only had two weeks to a well-earned retirement. He had reached that 'I don't give a fuck' stage, but he was still a cracking bobby. I had a lot of t ime for him.

"No problem, Terry," he said. "I've got the interpreters on standby," he laughed, "bearing in mind that half these Poles speak better fucking English than us lot."

The only one under arrest at the time was Jar, but that could change, we could use the other four as witnesses because, as sure is eggs is eggs, their passports would be amongst those we found in the safe.

Colin and the squad processed Jar and the four youngsters in the Custody suite whilst myself, Steve and Mike checked the property.

I was more interested in the passports at that time, there were nine. We flicked through them and noted the details and listed them as they came off the pile.

1. *Halina ADAMSKI...19 years of age*

2. *Ania GORSKI...19 years of age*

3. *Brygida DbBROWSKI.18 years of age*

4. *Rosanna BALCOFF... R.I.P.*

5. *Jarek BORKOWSKI...40 years of age*

6. *Ales BANURA...aged 20 years*

7. *Amadei PLUTA...aged 20 years*

8. Cezar ANTONIK...aged 22 years

9. Dawid BACHA...aged 21 years

"I think they call this a nap-hand, boys, what do you reckon?" I said.

Colin said, "Too fucking royal, boss. I'll have one of the boys to test the powder before it goes to the lab for comparison, and I'll have the SOCO's to check the passports for prints."

"I've got a feeling that Jar's trafficking and dealing days are done. I feel sorry for these youngsters," I admitted. "I'll get the boys to interview them and see exactly what's been going on. I bet they'll be glad they're free from the clutches of the beardy-bastard. Hopefully, we can trace the three other young girls."

"God knows what he's done to them? We may never find them, boss," Mike said.

I feared he might be right.

"I reckon we've prevented a few more kids ending up like bags of rubbish in the division. I just hope we can find the three girls before it's too late."

I poked the bag of powder with the end of my pen. "There must be about half a kilo there? I'm glad that hasn't hit our streets.

"Death and fucking Depravity, Mike, that's what this is, butt."

INTERVIEWS

I gave the custody suite a bell to ask Mal' how things were going with Jar and the four youngsters.

"The main-man is banged-up and the four youngsters have also now been arrested and detained on suspicion of supplying," he said.

I knew we now had the young lads for a minimum of thirty-six hours, and it was my intention to use them as witnesses against Jar. I felt sorry for the kids. They were probably just as much victims in all this as anyone, well, perhaps not everyone. I couldn't forget poor Rosanna who really pulled the short straw from all this shit.

Mal' went on to tell me that the four youngsters seemed relieved, and he could sense that they were terrified of Jar.

Mal' had years of experience behind him and was as sharp as Katie Hopkins' tongue. He told me he'd look after the youngsters and keep them sweet.

"Have they asked for interpreters?" I said.

"Only the one named Dawid Bacha. The rest are pretty sweet. It's all in hand, boss, and the immigration lot have been informed as well, just to be on the safe side."

"What about a brief for Jar?" I asked.

"I got him the duty solicitor, Ter,' he'll be here in about an hour. Have a guess who it is?" he snorted.

"Don't tell me, Mal.' It's that fat barrel of lard, Rod' Hughes?" we both had a chuckle, I knew Mal' hated Rod' with a passion.

"Send the squad boys back up to main office for de-brief, will you, Mal?"

"No problem, Ter,'" he said. "Fair play to your boys, they've been giving us a hand, just about finished here."

Within ten minutes, the gang was all gathered together.

I thanked them all for a job well done. I'm always keen to get the priorities right and a small word of thanks always went a long way, at least it did for me when I was in their shoes. I always remember my dad telling me many times; 'always be nice on your way up the ladder because everyone will queue up to piss and shit on you as you slide back down.' I've seen a similar quote somewhere else since my dad's days and the saying wasn't exactly like dad had told it to me. Still, I liked dad's version better.

All my team were now aware as to what had been recovered at the car wash office and it was obvious from Jar's actions, and all the gear, that he was running the show.

I could imagine the twat with the youngsters, probably paid them a pittance, got them hooked on shit and then pimped the young girls out. He was an evil, devious bastard.

I took centre stage. "First thing..." I said to Steve and Colin, "That bastard, Jar is yours. He can speak English so get stuck into him. I want to know about the girls, the drugs, the fucking lot. He'll probably go 'no comment,' especially with that fat, bent bastard, Rod-the-slimy-twat advising him. Don't take any shit off him. Any problem with Rod' and you give me a shout. I want to know where Jar lives and I want the place turned over. I also want to know where the girls are, if they're alive, dead or have been passed on? This is top priority. As for the four youngsters? Steve,' I want you to allocate two of the squad to each one of them and find out exactly what's been going on. I don't want any ambiguity. No place for guessing. Tie it down tight. You know the drill, where have they been living, how long they have been over here? Let's see if we can get a better picture of what's been going on. We know from Horace that it's been at least a twelve-month. The only one who needs an interpreter is Bacha, and Mal' is sorting that out.

"We'll have the passports checked for prints and the same with the packaging on the drugs. I bet a million fucking dollars that big Polish twat's dabs will be on them all. The clock is ticking and if things go to plan, we'll be able to charge him later on tomorrow.

"One other thing," I said, "try and get a connection between all the dead kids. We had nothing off the mobiles."

I turned to Steve, "Did Jar have a mobile on him when he was arrested?"

"Yes, boss, it's in his property," he said.

"Get it out, Steve, and give it to Jeff. He knows the drill. Perhaps we can glean something off it. We've got to know where those girls are."

I could see the rest of the team were worried for the missing girls. There were some pretty ugly, grim expressions in the room.

"Well done, everybody. Now crack on and let's put this to bed double quick. Do your best this evening and we'll have a de-brief about ten, before they're all bedded down for the night.

I got a call to tell me that Rod' Hughes had turned up and Jar was ready for interview. The four young lads didn't want briefs but the interpreter was also available.

To get a cough out of Jar would be nigh on impossible. I knew the type.

I watched my team leave to do the business on the youngsters. There was a real buzz of excitement in the room.

A few hours later, the squad came back into the office in dribs and drabs until they were all accounted for and the initial interviews had been completed.

"Is he talking, boys, or is it like we discussed earlier?" I asked Steve.

"You were spot on, boss, like Mystic fucking Meg, you are. No comment all the way through. We showed him the exhibits, the drugs, the passports, the cash. He just growled at us."

"He's a real mean bastard, boss," Colin added. "We're not going to get a lot out of him, but we've tied him tight on interview."

I thought about that for a moment. A full cough to the offences was always a surprise. I hadn't expected Jar to cough but it would have been nice, even though I really didn't think we needed it. "That's fair enough," I said. "I reckon we've got more than enough. I don't give a fuck if he stays mute for the next ten to fifteen years, because that's what he's looking at."

Then I remembered the Duty Solicitor. "Where's Rod' now?"

Colin grinned. "Still in the Custody suite, trying to get him bail but Mal' is having none of it. Jar's not going anywhere."

"What about the youngsters, can they throw any light on where this twat lives? And what about the girls, where have they all been living?"

"Boss, these kids are fucking terrified of Jar," Churchy told me. "Jar's one ruthless bastard. Seems like they've all been sleeping at the car wash. He pays them peanuts and knocks 'em about, always threatening to chuck them in the van and just dump them somewhere. Of course he keeps their passports so the poor fuckers can't go anywhere."

"How long have they been in the country, Churchy?"

"About a twelve month, perhaps a bit less, boss? They left Poland and were directed to Maesteg. I can't imagine anyone wanting to deliberately travel from Poland to Maesteg? Or they must have one hell of a holiday brochure they're touting around in Poland," he smiled.

"Travelling with Thomas Crook," one of the lads laughed.

"Certainly not fucking Virgin Travel," said another.

"Okay, okay," I grinned.

"I reckon these kids are being sent over to order," Churchy continued, "and he just pimps the girls out and works the youngsters like dogs. Then again, would you treat any dog like this? He's just scum, boss."

"So that's all we've got, is it?" I said as I walked to the coffee machine for my fix. "Okay, wrap it up, I'll see you all back at the office at eight am sharp. Go home and get some rest, perhaps a good night's kip and some hot grub in the cells will make the youngsters a bit more amenable? I'll go down and put Mal' in the picture. I think there's more to come."

I wished them all good night and they left the Bridewell Holding Centre.

I strolled down to the custody area, the hot coffee perked me up and I began to feel confident that we'd get this pile of shit sorted.

As I entered the corridor leading to the suite, I saw Mal' have, what could loosely be described as, a 'discussion,' with that big tub of lard Rod.' Mal' had Rod' by the lapels of his leather coat and was holding him up against the wall. Rod' was visibly shaking and Mal' was screaming, "You bent bastard, you wouldn't fucking lace his boots, you better apologise or by fuck I'll stick the head to you, you fucker."

I had never ever seen Mal' behave like this, and I have seen him deal with some real awkward bastards.

I got between them and pulled them apart

I ushered Mal' towards the Custody suite door and away from the slimy solicitor. By this time, Rod' was trying to say something. I had to lean in closer to hear. "I will have him…s..s..sacked, he's a disgrace," he stuttered.

Mal' had only taken a couple of paces when he turned on his heel and tried to grab Rod' by the throat.

Had it not been so serious I'd have laughed. I managed to usher Rod' into a side room and then made Mal' piss off into the custody suite.

I joined Rod' in the room, he was sweating profusely and dabbing his forehead with his red silk hankie, which was normally in the top pocket of his coat.

"I want him sacked, Chief Inspector, that's no way for a law enforcement officer to behave."

"Hey, fucking cool down. What did you say to him to make him react like that?"

Rod' looked insulted, clearly not used to his word being challenged. "What do you mean, what did I say?"

"Like I said, what did you fucking say?"

He looked unsure of himself, something I hadn't seen before. "I made an aside remark, that's all," he said.

"What did you say?" I asked more firmly.

He tried to smile. "I only made a bloody joke. A joke, that's all it was…"

"What did you say?" I growled menacingly.

"I said, I hope Terry isn't taking leaves out of the 'Cliff Ambrose journal of fit-ups' with this one…it was a joke, that's all and he just went berserk." The strength had returned to his voice. He folded his arms with attitude. "I want him sacked. I want to see the Inspector to lodge a formal complaint…"

"You fucking what? You fat twat. Make a complaint?

"Don't you dare speak to me like that…"

"Listen" I said, "how many of my prisoners have you represented over the years?"

He didn't have to think. "Many, Chief Inspector."

"Well, let me tell you now, Roddy boy. I know for a fact that you like the odd line of coke, because some of your clients have told me. You also like them young, and by that I mean young – boys, girls - and some of your clients have told me that as well. So let's not beat about the bush…you complain and I'll make fucking sure that your name is plastered all over the local papers. People will not go near you with a fucking bargepole; your reputation will be in tatters. You're a drug consuming, fucking pervert Rod,' end of. We tolerate you only because we don't want to bring disgrace on your profession. Now this is what's going to happen. You will apologise to Malcolm Old for the remark and we'll draw a line under it. Any comment you want to make? Or will it be 'no reply,' like you advise all your fucking morons?"

"You can't make allegations like that against me…that's offensive…"

"Yes it it. It's offensive because you're fucking offensive. Don't test me on this," I snarled.

"You would do that, Chief Inspector?"

"Too fucking royal I would. Now, is it a deal?"

I took the lack of reply as being good enough for me. I ushered Rod' towards the Custody Suite door, pressed the buzzer and a few seconds later Mal' appeared. His face flushed red again and I thought, for one awful moment that Mal' was going to give him a Glasgow Kiss. Thankfully, he caught my eye and stood off.

"Sergeant Old, I understand Mr Hughes has something to say to you," I said.

Rod' cleared his throat. "I am sorry if I caused any offence with my earlier remark, Sergeant? I apologise, and wish you well in your retirement."

All Mal' could manage was a curt nod before he turned and shut the door.

Rod' looked affronted but he said nothing. Good enough, you fat, bent bastard, I thought.

I got rid of Rod' and then I rung the buzzer again and Mal' appeared once more.

"You okay, Mal'?

He stood aside and let me enter the custody suite. "Yeah, he was out of order with that remark Terry, I just lost it."

"No problem, Mal,' thank you for defending my honour," we both laughed.

"I'm back in the morning Terry, I'll look after the youngsters for you."

We shook hands and I left for home, another long but productive day.

Mind you I didn't think Molly would see it that way.

Molly and Chris were both in bed by the time I got home.

I cracked open a can of beer, sat opposite the telly and watched a little crap on mute for an hour before I crept into bed.

I awoke early Wednesday morning. I had a long day ahead of me and needed an early start. I was gone from the house before there was any sign of movement from my family.

INTERVIEW WITH GERRY MURPHY

As a result of Steve Diamond's phone call last Friday, I got in touch with the Governor of Dartmoor Prison to see if Gerry Murphy would agree to speak with me.

Within the hour he was ringing me back, fair play, telling me that Murphy had agreed, and I could visit any time that was convenient to me.

I fixed the appointment for ten a.m. and wondered whether or not this would be a wild goose chase.

I arrived at the prison Wednesday morning, as arranged, and was greeted by the Governor, he shook my hand and welcomed me once again, "You must like it here, Terry? I hope you've put a good review on Trip Advisor?"

I laughed and he walked with me to the interview room, not that I needed guidance after all the visits I'd made of late. I thought this is becoming a bit of a fucking habit, now I knew what the term 'stir crazy' meant.

Murphy was already sitting in the Interview room and as soon as he saw me he smiled. "Fuck me, Terry, long time no see. Must be about ten years, surely?"

"Probably a bit longer," I said, but couldn't really recall the last meeting. It had been awhile. "How are things, Gerry, what you in for this time?"

He sucked through his teeth. Watched too many ghetto movies I thought. "Attempted robbery in Llan. I was off my face on coke and tried to rob the post office. I didn't account for the Post Master being a fucking hero; he was like fucking Bruce Lee and dropped me on the fucking spot. Took the replica off me. I end up with a five stretch, and he had a fucking medal, but there you go, win a few, lose a few more. At the moment I'm losing way more than I'm fucking winning, Terry. I'm being shunted all over the fucking country. I hope this is the last fucking move until I finish my bird."

"You never were the sharpest tool in the box, Gerry, let's be fair, and always off your face. I always thought you'd be found with a needle up your arm."

"No 'H for me, Terry boy, strictly speed or coke, that's been my motto."

A little sharper than I originally thought, but still blunter than a plastic knife.

"Right, Gerry, let's get down to business. What you got for me?"

"Oh, the old murder, is it, Terry? Yeah, I know who did that."

"And please do tell, good sir."

I was expecting him to lay out a list of 'wants' in exchange for the name but was surprised when he just blurted it out. "Mike Foley, a local boy from Bridgend." He sat back in his chair and crossed him arms – job done. I took a new pack of JPS Silver's from my pocket, a brand the Governor had told me Murphy was partial to, and I raised my eyes at the guard hovering in the background for permission to light one for my new best friend. I got the nod and lit one for him and passed it across the table.

"Too kind, good sir," he mocked my earlier comment.

I smiled. "Tell me more. Let me warn you, before you start, you had better not be taking the fucking piss? I haven't driven all this way for a load of shite, so have a good think."

He blew a cloud of smoke into the enclosed space and added a couple of smoke rings to impress. "No need, Terry, this is straight up. He's done well to get away with it for as long as this…what, twenty odd years?"

I shrugged, pretending I wasn't sure of whom he was referring to.

"The bloke he did was a twat, perhaps that's why he's still out?"

I leaned forward onto the table, closing the space between us. "Start from the beginning, Gerry, chapter and verse, butt."

He took another long draw on his cigarette and coughed. "The bloke he did was Ken Porter," he looked at me as if I should know him. I didn't give anything away. "He had a second hand shop in Pontycymer?" I still stayed silent. "Bit of a money lender come handler who also did a bit of supplying, nothing heavy, speed and blow and only to a selected few. I suppose you could say he was…discerning?"

"Did you have any dealings with him?"

"Oh aye…"

"Thought you said he was discerning?" I cracked.

Murphy laughed. "I was one of his customers, but he was a smarmy bastard. When it came over the news that he'd been done, you would swear he was fucking Snow White. Terry, he was a shit and no loss to the valley."

"That's beside the point, Gerry, he was a human being...and just think what pain those seven dwarfs must have gone through at the news of their loss."

He didn't bite. "Human fucking being? Christ alive, Terry, you going soft or what?"

"Always been known for my empathy, mate."

"Look, Terry, you know what they're like in the valleys...tight, like shit to a blanket with their own...but the likes of Porter? They couldn't give a fuck about him."

"What about Foley, what's the connection?"

"Well, like I said, I was a customer, and so was Foley. I used to pay up front but Foley would have gear on the knock, you know, have now, pay later, a credit agreement, you might say?"

"Just like the banks, eh? Get you in a state of need and then pull the plug?"

He smiled. "You got it. Peter was a clever twat like that. If you owed him, he had you by the bollocks. Some were doing breaks to order for him and that's how they would pay him off. Foley definitely owed him…big time. I knew that for a fact."

"What's Foley's background, Gerry?"

"Worked underground in the Ffaldau pit, up until the 84 strike, and then went self-employed as a mechanic, worked from the garage behind his house in Bridgend until his missus fucked off with the kids.

"He was doing well. Many of the locals had their cars serviced with him, but, like anything else, the old habit ate into his wages.

"I know they were really fucked by the strike. Really hard up. His old girl even had to do some tricks for money, so she couldn't really say anything to Mike about his habit, other than he was wasting what little dosh they had. His missus was smart, mind, a real looker, lovely pair of pins and tits to die for. She upped-sticks and left him on his own. Think he still is? I haven't seen him for a few years."

"Gerry, I want some evidence, not fucking rumour and guess-work. Do you know for definite that he killed Porter?"

"For fuck sake, Terry, he told me many years ago that he did it. Told me that he hadn't even been interviewed about it."

"Did he tell you how and why he killed him?"

"Well, that's fucking obvious, Terry. He owed Porter big time. All he told me was that he battered him with a ballpein hammer and fucking dumped him in the forestry over Maesteg way. I think you'll find that the body wasn't found for a couple of days?"

"What about Porter's van?"

"Every fucker knows that was dumped not far from Bettws, the place was alive with coppers, I remember it well."

"Why would he tell you this, and incriminate himself in a brutal murder, Gerry. Doesn't seem very sensible considering he was away, Scott-free."

He held his hand out for another smoke so I lit another and passed it over.

"You know what it's like, Terry, when you're off your face anything goes. We were out on the piss one night and he just blurted it out."

"Just like that?"

He nodded his head as he enjoyed the smoke. "Pretty much, yeah. I tried speaking to him about it a few days later, but he wasn't playing ball, so I didn't push it."

"I'm surprised you can remember, Gerry, your fucking head must have been fried at the time? You were Bridgend's fucking answer to Ronnie Wood."

"Don't be fucking smarmy, Terry, this is straight up." He took a long drag on his smoke. "How you prove it? Well, I don't know about that. I'm not the fucking copper in the room."

I sat back. "Why are you saying this now, Gerry, like twenty odd years later?"

"The older you get the wiser, in'it, Terry?"

"So this is the new wiser Gerry Murphey talking?"

He shrugged and sucked through his teeth again. "I have no doubt there may be a few bob in it, should you do the business. Mind you, I'm not talking to any other fucker, only you."

"Would you give evidence, if this all pans out?"

"Aye, why not? I've always liked that saying, you know…'I will have my day in court,' like in the witness box for a change and not the fucking dock."

"Fair play, Gerry, you haven't lost your sense of humour, I always liked that about you."

"This bloke Foley got any form? I asked.

"No, not that I know. I think he's clean as a whistle, Terry. I reckon you could get him on DNA."

"Fuck me, Gerry, you've been watching too much C.S.I. on the box. This could very well be down to a cough, if it gets that far."

"I reckon you could crack him, Terry, I don't think it would take much to be honest."

"Oh aye, Gerry? Put yourself in Foley's shoes, I come knocking on your door, twenty one years after the fact, arrest you for murder and you cough it in the back of the car on the way to the nick. *'It's a fair cop, guv, it's me what done it,'* I don't fucking think so."

"Aye, I see where you're coming from, Terry. I wouldn't fucking have it either, you'll have to crack him on his alibi."

I held up my hand. "Enough now, Gerry, you're getting on my fucking nerves. I didn't know you had a degree in criminology."

Gerry chuckled. "We're in the same business, just different sides of it, Terry."

I sighed. "I'll have a look into it, but I don't hold out much hope. Perhaps you should have come forward when the murder took place?"

"Hindsight's a wonderful thing, Terry, isn't it, butt? Anyway, why would I? The roots of education are bitter, but the fucking fruit is lush, butt."

I was gobsmacked. "Fuck me, Gerry, didn't know your middle name was Aristotle?"

"Wisdom finds many…"

I stopped the daft twat in his tracks. "Hold on…hold on. No more of that shit. Closest you'd ever get to wisdom is Norman Wisdom, and he's dead. Now, Mr Grimsdale, let's put all this bollocks on paper." I fished in my coat pocket and pulled out two-hundred smokes. "Here's a couple of packs for you."

I then spent the next two hours taking Gerry's witness statement, wondering what the fuck I was doing? The case had been reviewed a few times and I was sure something like this would have stood out a mile, but then again, who knows these days?

I really didn't want to get involved in it, but I thought It wouldn't hurt to run it up the ACC's pole and see if it would flutter. Being the sharp fucker he is, I knew the ACC would probably tell me to investigate because of the drugs involved.

After I finished with Gerry, I made my way back to the Governor's office and had a cup of coffee and chewed the fat. Our conversation quickly deteriorated into a mutual moan as we slagged-off every senior officer in the Police and Prison service.

Feeling better after the moan, I shook the Governors hand and made my way to the car. I liked the Governor, we were almost besties.

I thought I'd give the ACC a bell, just to run it by him. As luck would have it he was in the office and his secretary put me through.

I brought him up to speed on the information, and, as I suspected, he gave me a free hand to investigate the matter, "If it's been reviewed a few times, there's nothing to lose, is there, Terry?" he said. "Do you need any extra bodies for this one?"

I thought about it. "Only a couple to go through the old files and exhibits. I was thinking of John Fuller off SB and young Caroline Williams, the young aide from Bridgend. I'll throw in one of my own, DC Karen Fitzgerald."

"They're yours, Terry, first thing in the morning, leave it with me."

I thanked the ACC and made my way back home. My mind was racing far quicker than I was driving the Ford Focus, but this is what police work was all about, and it's why I loved it.

The evening at home was a lovely change. I managed to spend time with Molly and Chris and we talked about the engineering project that Chris had secured, a project that looked likely to pave the way to many more major construction jobs in Asia. That meant Chris was on the verge of making some serious money. I was pleased for him but I still wanted him home. I wanted both my kids at home but knew they had to find their own way in life, wherever that may take them.

We sank a lovely bottle of red I picked up on my way home and I don't think Molly stopped smiling the entire night. I wanted the evening to last forever but knew that my life and my work would always conspire to throw the odd spanner into the works. I couldn't fully relax, I never can when I'm at home, I'm always expecting that call, that big spanner to crash through and spoil things. As it happened, I needed have worried, at least not until the morning.

THE REVELATION

I was washing up my breakfast dishes when the phone rang. I admit that the first thought that went through my mind was that I might escape doing the bloody dishes. I hate doing it. The dishwasher had been on the blink for a few weeks and had added more strength to Molly's argument for a new kitchen.

"Hello? Terry here."

It was Malcolm Old.

"Sorry to bother you, Terry, but you've got to get someone down the Bridewell as soon as. "

All sorts of things went through my mind, had Jar topped himself like Cliff Ambrose? That would fuck things up big time. Had something happened to one of the youngsters?

"What's happened, Mal'?"

"Well, you know I said that I'd keep them sweet? Well the young lad Banura wants to speak to someone."

"What about, Mal'?"

"He's saying that Jar has killed one of the girls and she's buried up at the car wash."

Well I was speechless. I couldn't believe it. I composed myself and told Mal I would be there as soon as.

I knew the interview teams would be in at eight, so there was no real problem.

I put the phone down, grabbed a piece of toast, apologised to Molly and Chris and was out of the door like Superman on a mission, but without the colourful underwear.

I heard Chris, laugh, "There he goes again, the one man crime busting machine."

Sarcasm from my son? They had every right to be, it hadn't been the first time they had seen me behave like this and I had no doubt it wouldn't be the last.

I got to the Bridewell about twenty minutes later and conferred with Mal.'

"What do you reckon, Mal,' is he on the up?"

"I think so, Ter,' he's shit-scared, butt. I've assured him you'll look after him and his butties...you will, won't you?"

I nodded earnestly. "Of course I will, Mal,' if this is on the up, that bastard will not see the light of day again. Look, when the boys come in, I'll sort out the interview, you okay with that?"

"No problem, Terry."

"I owe you big time," I told my old mate. "I think this is on a par with you throttling Rod.'"

Mal' managed to force a laugh, he knew he had come close to losing his pension when he throttled the slime-bag and I shook his hand. He was a real diamond in the rough.

The interview teams assembled a short while later, together with Colin and Steve.

I informed them of the latest development and asked who had interviewed the young lad called Banura?

Chris Graham and Mark Morgan, raised their hands in unison, "We did, boss," Mark said.

"How did you find him, boys?"

"Shit scared to be honest, boss," Mark told me. "You could tell he was hiding things, can't blame him, to be honest, in view of this."

"Listen now you two, I want you to get back into him, he'll talk. Go down have a chat with Sgt Old and do the business. Just get me the guts of it all so we can move on with this. If this is right it will be a cracking breakthrough, now go and do the business."

Normally I would have had either a DI or a DS to do the interview but I am not normal and I want to give people a chance to learn the right way.

Chris and Mark were out of the traps like greyhounds on steroids.

I then got hold of Mike in the office and told him to send the remainder of the squad up to the car wash in Maesteg to preserve the scene and to also get S.O.C. there as well. I wanted Glyn Walcott out; if this was on the up I wanted the best man on it.

I knew the next couple of hours would drag. Even though I wasn't involved in the interview, I was there in spirit, willing the boys on, hoping they will do the business for me.

I give my mate Detective Superintendent Wyn Croak, 'Major Crime,' a ring and told him about the information that we'd received.

Wyn is experienced, a good egg, a proper detective.

"I'll put my team on standby," he told me. No point in causing a Kerfuffle if there was bugger-all in it.

A couple of hour later, Chris and Mark bound into the office, hyped and smiling.

"Boss, Jar's fucking strangled the girl and buried her in concrete in the inspection pit at the garage."

"Do we know which girl it is?"

"Yes, " he said. "Ales says it's Halina."

"Fuck, she's on the list."

"Well, it was about four months ago, apparently. This fucking Jar bloke was in the office with her, there was a big argument, over what Banura doesn't know. He saw him grab the girl around the throat and start shaking her. One minute she was standing there, being strangled and the next Banura couldn't see her. He ran to the office and saw her, lifeless on the floor. Jar was standing over Halina and he screamed at

Banura to get out, to shut all the forecourt lights off and get rid of all the cars.

"Banura shit himself and did what he was told.

"Boss, this fucking bloke is a psychopath," Chris said.

"Anyway," Mark continues, "once all the cars are gone, he calls the four of them in and has them carry Halina's body into the garage. Jar followed with black bin bags and duct tape. The bastard trussed her up in the bin bags and then dropped her into the inspection pit with all the other rubbish, oil cans, bits of old cars, food cartons and other shit.

"He warned them all to keep their mouths shut, or they'd join her."

"What happened next, boys?"

"The following day, he shut the place and got bags of ready-mix concrete and just fucking covered her over, she's about two feet deep, boss.

Banura will take us up there and show us. He'll also show us where Jar lives, he doesn't know the actual address but he can show us the house, it's no far from the car wash."

"Where have these four lads been living?"

"They doss at the car wash or with Jar, he has a hold over them, boss, I feel fucking sorry for them, and the girls."

"If this can happen around here and we don't know about it, what the fuck is happening countrywide?" I said. "What about the other girls and the drugs, anything on that?"

"All he knows is that Jar gets them hooked on the dope and he pimps them out. They only see them now and again, usually when they first come on the scene. He seems to think that Jar picks them up and drops them in different places where they knock out the gear and basically sell their bodies. Jar pockets all the cash. It's a fucking nightmare boss."

"Well done, boys. Now let's get this show on the road."

I ring Wyn again and he tells me that he will confer with me at the scene in half an hour and, depending on what's found, he'll get his team out and open an incident room at Maesteg nick.

I also get hold of Jeff to get a search team on standby with all the necessary tools to break concrete.

The next stop is the car wash premises. I tell Chris and Mark to get Ales Banura ready for the ride of his life.

The four of us then make our way to the car wash. Part of me is hoping the body is there, so we can throw the key away on Jar and the other part is hoping it's not another one. It never gets easier and I know a part of my soul is snipped away each time I think like this.

HALINA ADAMSKI

We arrived at the car wash to find it all taped off, with uniform staff ensuring that all the main road traffic was flowing freely and there was no 'rubber necking' taking place.

Chris drove with me in the front seat and I'd brought Mark and the young lad, Ales with us. He sat in the back of the car whilst I conferred with Wyn, Gwyn Walcott and Inspector Millman, the search coordinator, and discussed the way forward,

Gwyn was dressed in his all whites, with facemask accessory. A photographic negative, and nicer, version of Darth Vader.

He informed us that he'd gone over the office with a fine toothcomb and had bagged a few exhibits, including a roll of silver duct tape.

The garage and showroom area didn't look all that big from the outside. The showroom windows had been blacked out, and I had no doubt that the area inside was quite expansive, with the usual offices, toilets and store rooms.

It was decided that the search team and Glyn would be the only officers at this stage to actually venture inside, it was paramount that everything was photographed in situ' and that the area around the inspection pit was sterile.

Wyn gave the instructions to Gwyn, the Inspector, and the search team, who were tooled up with small Kango hammers, shovels and picks.

"Best of luck, lads. Let us know when you find something."

Wyn turned to me, "I've got Doc' Powell on speed dial Terry, I've already had a chat. If the boys find anything, he'll be with us in fifteen minutes, so keep your fingers crossed. I'm going back to Maesteg nick. They could be a while here."

I nodded my head and got back in the car.

***

Two officers dressed in white coveralls, ear defenders and masks, descended carefully down into the concrete vehicle inspection pit. Built to allow mechanics access to the underbody of vehicles, the pit was no more than a concrete-lined rectangular pit. The car would drive over it and a set of steps would allow the mechanic access.

The bottom was littered with empty drink cans, food-wrappers, newspapers and someone had even used it as an impromptu toilet. It stank of ammonia and shit.

Two small but heavy Kango hammers were lowered down to the officers and the mobile generator started to power the hammers.

The broad-tipped chisel blades make quick work of the thin layer of concrete that had seemingly been added much later than the rest of the pit had been built.

Glyn watched carefully, four high-powered lights on telescopic stands lit the pit better than daylight. "Stop!" Glyn shouted.

The two officers stopped digging and stood still.

Glyn pointed to one end, "Look, there…"

The officer closet placed his Kango in the top of the pit and bent down to take a closer look.

Glyn watched as the officer carefully removed the broken concrete. He then stopped and turned to look at Glyn. "We found her."

***

"Can you take us to where Jar lived?" I asked Ales.

He nodded and then directed Chris as we travelled along the main road towards Bridgend, through Garth and down towards Llangynwyd. We turned right and then left into Heol Tyn Y Waun. We stopped outside number 22, a small bungalow, from the outside I guessed it to be a two bedroom.

The front curtains were drawn. Mark got out and had a quick look around, "It's all secure, boss. All the curtains are pulled closed, can't see in at all."

"Okay, Mark," I said, "you stay here, do a bit of house to house and see if you can glean anything from the neighbours. I'll sort out a search authority and get a few of the boys and a SOCO and you can all do the business. Shouldn't take long."

"No problem, boss, leave it with me."

I was thinking of how I would have handled this a couple of years ago. I would have smashed the fucking door off the hinges, but times had changed, everything now seemed to be weighted for the criminal and their human rights. In my book, this fucker gave up on his human rights when he strangled that poor girl and dumped her like fucking garbage.

We then made our way back to the nick at Maesteg.

We made Ales comfortable. Chris stayed with him, and at the same time subtly pumped him for more information.

I rang Jeff to get a couple of the lads to confer with Mark down in Llan and do the business on the bungalow.

I then had a coffee with Wyn and we chatted about the old times, how things had changed, not for the better, the usual bollocks old-sweats spouted whenever they got together.

Then I remembered I had to sort out the search authority. Nearly forgot. I rang the duty Inspector at the Bridewell, explained the situation, and he sorted it straight away, no questions asked.

Within the hour, my mobile rang, it was Glyn.

"We got her boss, she wasn't down more than a fucking foot, trussed up like a turkey, I have taken some shots, but I'll wait for the Home Office Pathologist."

I informed Wyn and he, in turn, called his team out to set up the Incident Room, together with a mobile version down at the scene. He also called out Doc' Powell.

Even though everything had come together nicely, it still rankled with me. It was no way for a young girl to die. Jar had a lot to answer for.

Myself and Wyn made our way to the car wash and suited up, - clones of Darth - we then made our way into the area of the inspection pit.

Poor Halina was lying in the bottom, someone's little girl, surrounded by rubble, wrapped in black bin liners stuck together with grey duct tape. All I could see of her was a small face that had once been pretty, framed by curly blonde hair. She looked peaceful, bearing in mind the manner in which she had met her end.

Within fifteen minutes, Doc' Powell made his appearance. We brought him up to speed and he made a cursory examination of Halina. I waited for him to finish.

"Pretty obvious, cause of death was manual strangulation, there's finger bruising around her neck and a great deal of force has been used. Once I do the PM, I'll be able to tell you more. I'll do it first thing in the morning. Is that okay for you, boys? There's enough for you to get on with, no doubt, a decent starter for ten."

I thanked the Doc' and arrangements were then made for the body to be conveyed to the mortuary at the Princess of Wales Hospital.

We left Gwyn there with his team to top and tail it all and once the body had been removed the premises could then be secured and a Police presence would remain there until further notice.

Myself and Wyn then made our way back to the nick. I was beginning to feel sick of all the travelling I was doing. When we got there it was a hive of activity.

The major crime team were setting up the incident room, and getting it all prepared for a full-on murder enquiry.

In the meantime, Mark had returned after searching the bungalow and reported that there wasn't much there, quite Spartan, some drug paraphernalia, syringes burnt spoons, the usual toys of doom, but no documentation whatsoever.

He had found an unlocked padlock and hasp on the door and frame of the small bedroom and a couple of mattresses on the floor.

"Well, we all know what that was for, don't we?" I said.

"Anything from the neighbours," I asked Mark.

"I did a few, boss, but it'll need a full house-to-house."

"Leave that to my, boys," Wyn said. "I think your team have done enough, a cracking result."

Wyn then took me to one side, "I'm calling a briefing at seven. I want you to brief my team, the full kit and caboodle. As it's a murder, I'll be the SIO and I'll take it over. I'll liaise with Immigration and all other agencies that may be involved, are you okay with that, Terry?"

"I have no problem with that at all, Wyn, but you'll look after the four youngsters? Promise me."

"Leave them to me, Terry, I'll have them put up in a safe house for the duration, you have no worries on that score. As for the other two girls, I'll try my best to trace them, but you know the chances are slim, especially if this fucking lunatic has been running them."

Contrary to what I've often seen in police dramas from the States, there's no jurisdictional animosity between departments in our force. We all recognise the importance of our roles and the strengths of each. There are always the odd senior twat that can make things awkward but, on the whole, everything is pretty good humoured.

Seven o'clock came and I briefed the Major Crime Unit and then left them to their work. I knew many of them personally, sound officers with a wealth of experience in this sort of enquiry.

Wyn shook my hand "That squad of yours are really doing the fucking business, you should be proud of them, Terry."

"I am, I am." I thanked Wyn and I felt ten feet tall. The team had done me proud again.

I rang Jeff to get all the squad back to the office for a de-brief at eight.

Me, Chris, Mark and Ales then made our way to the Bridewell.

On the way I had a good chat with Ales and promised him that Wyn would look after them all.

At eight on the dot, the whole squad were in the office and I held centre stage, telling them that Major Crime had now taken the murder over together with the trafficking enquiries, which freed us all up to concentrate on what we're best at -arresting suppliers who are killing our kids.

I sent the team home for a rest. They'd worked hard and I needed them fresh.

I asked Mal, Steve and Colin to stay behind for a few minutes. I managed to find four glasses, opened my top draw, pulled out my bottle of malt, and poured some small ones. We toasted the squad and filled the glasses a second time to toast the poor unfortunate souls lost to death and debauchery.

THE COLD CASE

I was over the moon with the result of Operation GDANSK, it was satisfying to take any batch of drugs out of circulation but even more so when it was responsible for deaths.

On the downside, four young people had died unnecessarily.

The heroin that they had used to unwittingly overdose had definitely come from the same batch that was recovered from the car wash.

Major Crime had charged Jarek Borkowski, aka Jar, with the murder of poor Halina Adamski and was now on remand in Cardiff nick.

The four young Polish lads had made their witness statements and were being put up in a safe house until the trial, so that was a plus.

I had no doubt Jar would be further charged with more serious offences in relation to those deaths, again, another plus.

Alas, we couldn't trace Ania Gorski and Brygida Dnrowski, the two young Polish girls that Jar had pimped out.

Were they dead, or still plying their trade in some other part of the country, being shunted around like human garbage?

I had a gut feeling they were, in fact, dead, surplus to requirements in the growing trade of human trafficking, where young girls and boys are being used, abused and treated worse than animals. It was a sad indictment on today's society, this criminal behaviour was occurring right under our noses.

Anyway, we had to move on. The squad were out on the ground, doing what they did best, speaking to narks, and obtaining information on dealers.

I knew they were in good hands with Mal' and Chris. My time would now be taken up with the Porter murder.

Right on cue, my cold case team, consisting of D.C John Fuller from Special Branch, who was my right hand man on the Ambrose enquiry, Temporary DC Caroline Williams, off Division, a young and keen asset, and one of my own DC's Karen Fitzgerald, a HOLMES trained operator, appeared at my office door.

I needed Karen's specialist skills with the HOLMES system. HOLMES is an acronym for HOME OFFICE LARGE ENQUIRY SYSTEM and was an administrative support introduced in 1985. It enabled law enforcement agencies to improve effectiveness in serious criminal offences.

HOLMES processed the mass of information produced on major enquiries, ensuring that no vital clues would be lost.

I had heard it said that if it had been around when the Yorkshire Ripper was up to his antics he would have been arrested much sooner and lives would have been saved. At the time, the Ripper enquiry generated mountains of paperwork and everything had to be done manually. Tons of it filed and sifted and vital information inevitably missed.

Karen would pull up all the relevant information on the Porter case off HOLMES and we would take it from there.

"I've received information regarding an unsolved murder going back to Friday, the eleventh of August 1995," I told her.

"The victim was one Kenneth Porter, born on the first of the third 1950. Porter resided alone at 50, High Street, Pontycymer. He was the owner of the 'Garw Seconds,' shop in Oxford Street, Pontycymer. He dealt in second hand goods and also supplied drugs. He owned a Blue Ford Escort van reg' number Golf-Sierra-100.

"Porter's van was found abandoned on Thursday the tenth, at the bottom of Bettws Hill, near the village of Shwt.

"His body was found the following day, dumped in the forestry area near the old St John's Colliery. It was wrapped in tarpaulin with his skull caved in.

"I've specifically asked for you three to assist me with this investigation. I want you to go and trawl through all the information that HOLMES spews out. I'm particularly interested in suspects, sightings, exhibits and if there is DNA or fingerprint evidence that may link the suspect with the Murder? The suspect, at this moment in time, is Michael John Foley, born seventh of the eleventh 1955. He has no form whatsoever, but was being supplied with drugs by Porter on the knock. The informant says Foley owed Porter money for drugs but was never actually interviewed with regard to the murder.

"I also want you to find me a detective who worked closely with the two SIOs at the time of the murder; sadly the SIOs are now both deceased. Are there any questions?"

"Is the information sound, boss," John asked.

"To be honest with you, John, the case has been reviewed a couple of times without any progress, so does that answer your question?"

"Yes, boss, I can see where you're coming from."

"Aye, but the review team didn't have three coppers of your calibre, did they?" I grinned. "We'll look at it in a more pro-active way, you never know. Foley will be arrested one way or another, so it may come down to DNA and prints. Anyway, let's be positive about it all. Now, off you go, we'll have another briefing on Friday at eight, here in the office. Happy hunting. Before you go, Karen? See if you can give me the detective I asked for by the end of the day?"

"No problem, boss, you got it."

THE HATTONS

The last week had been hard on Molly and Chris, they had hardly seen me and I felt terrible about that, however, I was also thinking about another family, the Hattons.

They had lost two sons overnight, so I had some solace that Molly would understand my predicament. At least my two children were safe and well, and I   thanked God for that.

Peter Hardwick gave me the background on the Hatton's and they seemed like a hard working middle-class family and they must have been going through hell.

I decided it was time I paid them a visit, to give my condolences and to inform them about the enquiry.

I got hold of Jane and she accompanied me to Pencoed a village near Bridgend.

Pencoed is a typical Welsh community; it developed from the nineteenth century growth in coal mining, now those mines had gone and the town was perhaps now better known as the place dissected by the M4 at junction 35?

It's a nice place to live, a place many of my friends had lived in for most their lives. But with about nine-thousand people living there it was no surprise that I had never crossed paths with the Hatton's before.

We drove a short distance past the local precinct that housed the chippy, off-licence and laundrette and arrived at the Hatton's semi-detached house. It was a double-fronted red-brick box of a house, typical seventies build which sported later additions, such as white plastic windows and a red composite door set into a slope-roof porch at the front.

The front garden was laid to lawn that looked better than the greens on most golf courses I'd played and a brick-paved path led up to the red door.

I knocked and waited until a young man in his twenties answered.

"Can I help you?" he said.

I introduced Jane and myself and he smiled and invited us in, showing us through into the surprisingly spacious lounge. The sunken spots in the ceiling were on but were on a dimmed setting. The sense of loss in the room was palpable, I could see it, feel it, hear it and even smell it.

The house was spotlessly clean, well-furnished and decorated with taste; this was the home of a family with pride.

Mrs Hatton was sitting on the black leather settee, with her knees pulled up and tucked underneath her chin. It came as no surprise to see that she'd been crying, Mr Hatton kneeled on the floor alongside her, with his head resting on her shoulder.

The tall and good-looking young lad introduced us, and I gestured both of them to stay as they were. Jane and I shook both their hands as they sat and I offered our condolences.

They were already aware that their boys had died of a massive heroin overdose.

The family liaison had been with them for the first couple of days to support and offer some comfort.

Jane and I then sat on the easy chairs, and the young lad offered us tea or coffee. We declined.

Mrs Hatton dried her eyes and blew her nose. "Have you found out what happened, Chief Inspector?"

Mr Hatton looked at me with eyes that had seen more than a father should ever have to. "I understand there have been other deaths, similar to our Paul and Scott," he said flatly.

The tears rolled down his wife's face and Mr Hatton pulled her in close.

We said nothing. I felt so bad for them. To lose one child is a never-ending nightmare but to lose two together didn't bare thinking about.

Mr Hatton eventually nodded to the young lad standing in the doorway. "This is our eldest boy, Graham, he's twenty-two and all we have left, Chief Inspector."

I looked at Graham. "Make sure you look after each other?"

He nodded and cast his eyes to the ground.

"You're right," I said to the Hatton's, "there have been two other deaths in the area. I can tell you that your boys, and the two other youngsters, died as a result of using heroin from the same source, a source that wasn't far off from being pure. Sadly, it seems their young bodies couldn't cope with it."

"Have you caught the dealers?" Graham asked.

I nodded. "Yes, we've arrested the individual concerned and he's been charged with one count of murder, and other serious offences relating to the supplying of the heroin. I can't go into any detail at this time because of the pending court case.

Mr Hatton nodded his head then seemed to want to say something but struggled to get the words out. "Did…er…did our boys…did our boys suffer, Chief Inspector?"

I didn't really know the answer to that, I would only be guessing but I knew a little white lie wasn't going to cause anymore hurt to these good people. "No, Mr Hatton," I said with conviction. "It would have been a quick, painless passing."

He just sighed and nodded his head. I could see that the family were broken into pieces that would never be repaired and obviously wanted to be left alone to grieve.

I gave Jane the nod and we both stood up to leave.

Mrs Hatton rose slowly to her feet, she looked exhausted, her shoulders seemed to have lost their shape and she crossed her arms. I thought she looked as if she was hugging the memory of her dead children to her breast. "They weren't bad boys, were they, Chief Inspector? They weren't bad boys, were they?"

Jane put her arms around Mrs Hatton, cwtching her tightly. "Of course not, Mrs Hatton, of course not. They just made a silly mistake. They weren't to know."

Graham and Mr Hatton moved in closer and started comforting the distraught woman as Jane stepped away to leave the three sobbing together, trying to bury their heads in each other, to block out the world and seek solace where there was none to be found.

I left them huddling and placed my card on the mantelpiece, "If you need anything, anything at all, give me a call, any time, day or night."

I rarely gave my card to anyone, but I thought that in this case I would make an exception.

Mr Hatton broke from the huddle and he accompanied us to the front door.

He shook our hands, gave Jane a kiss on the cheek and sobbed as he thanked us for all that the Police had done.

He then closed the front door.

We were left standing there, looking at that blood-red door. People talk of closure, this family would never have that, and they would never be the same again.

Jane and I made our way back to the car; we were drained from a very unpleasant experience.

Jane drove back to the office as I sat quietly in the front. All sorts of thoughts bounced around in my head and all of them involved the Hatton's. I thought of two young boys I'd never known, running to the swings and playing with their toys. I thought of them running on the beach, splashing through waves and being carried by their mam and dad up the stairs to their bedroom, exhausted from the fun and dreaming of the bright future that lay ahead for them.

Sometimes life is just shit!

"You did well in there," I finally said.

I could see Jane shrug in my peripheral vision as I stared out through the front screen at a road that could have been anywhere, none of it registered.

"A little honest compassion can help a great deal…I like that."

"It was so sad," she said.

"I can see you having a fabulous career ahead of you" I said. "Now all we've got to do is get you promoted."

She forced a laugh, "If I do, boss, it will have to be back on to the bikes."

I cringed. "Don't know what you see in them? Bloody death traps."

"Nothing quite like it, boss. The bikes are safe enough, it's the other road users are the problem. Don't see us, some don't even look for us. But there's nothing like riding a motorbike at speed."

"Rather you than me," I said.

"It's at times like this I like to open the throttle and blast away the troubles of the day."

***

We entered the office and Jeff informed me that Karen had found a DS who had worked on the Porter murder, his name was Sean

Maddigan, retired about five years ago and still lived locally.

I got the Bridgend number from Jeff and a few minutes later I dialled and a bloke answered, "Four-four-four-one-six-four, can I help you?"

"Sean Maddigan, ex DS?" I said.

"Who wants to know?" The voice sounded suspicious.

"It's DCI Terry McGuire off the drug Squad. I'd like to speak to Sean if possible?"

"Terry McGuire? Ah yes, I've heard good reports about you, how can I help?"

"Sean, I'm re-investigating the Ken Porter murder back in 1995, I understand you worked on it?"

"Oh? Aye, I was on it alright. It was a fuck up from the start, Terry, too many egos amongst the top men, you know what it's like."

I did know, only too well. "Can we meet to have a chat about it, perhaps you can throw a bit of light on it for me, you know...how it was run, did they miss anything?"

"No problem, Terry, call around in the morning, you got my address, but you were lucky to catch me. The Mrs and me are flying to Madeira at six tomorrow evening. I'll certainly give you as much information as I can. Make it first thing, Terry about nine, is that ok?"

I gave Molly a ring straight after, telling her that I was on my way.

***

The meeting with the Hatton's had been traumatic. There was nothing worse than losing someone in such terribly tragic circumstances. It must have been dreadful for the officers who had called on them to tell them about the death of their two boys.

Jane thought about Terry's comments about promotion. She hadn't given it much thought but it had been in her long-term plans for a while now. She was enjoying herself on the Squad too much to accept the offer just now, but it made her feel good that her Chief thought so well of her.

She opened the throttle of her sleek, black 1100cc Yamaha Virago motorcycle. The front wheel lifted as the power transfer to the rear wheel thrust the cycle along the A48 towards Bridgend. It was a route she had ridden many times, especially during the many police motorcycle advanced and refresher course she had taken during her service.

She couldn't get Mrs Hatton's broken face out of her mind and she felt tears run down her cheeks inside her full-face helmet as she banked the bike low around a left hand bend, watching for the break point of the corner and then accelerating through the racing line that wasn't always police best practice on these roads.

The road straightened then began a long sweeping turn to the right. She knew a short straight followed and then another tight left. She made the final bend in short time and eased off for the tight left-hander.

There was nothing she could do. The articulated lorry had jack-knifed on the bend and was across the full width of the road. She closed her eyes and lay the bike down on its side. The slide towards the lorry was horrendous. She thought of her family and the tears they would shed, her colleagues, the laughs, the joy the fear, and of her boss, Terry. He wasn't going to be happy.

**

I got a call from the hospital, as I was about to leave for home. It was Ted Michaels, a traffic officer I'd joined the force with many years before.

"Terry? It's Ted. I'm afraid I've got some bad news for you. It's Jane, your DC?"

"What's happened, Ted? Is she okay?"

The line went silent for a brief moment. "I'm afraid she's dead. She was killed a couple of hours ago. Ran into a Jack-knifed..."

The rest of what Ted was saying faded away. It didn't matter. All that mattered was that Jane was dead, the woman I had recently spoken to about promotion, the woman who had shown great compassion for others, who had so much to live for.

I looked across the office and could see Jeff speaking on another line. His face was ashen and his mouth hung open. I guessed he was receiving the news too.

I hung up and walked over to Jeff. He dropped the receiver and stood, his hands were moving, so too was his mouth but nothing was said. I grabbed him by the shoulders and hugged him tight. We both stood there for God knows how long, tears streaming down our faces.

A BLAST FROM THE PAST

I turned up at the home of Sean Maddigan, as arranged, and was welcomed by a very smartly dressed and self-assured individual. I shook his hand and he led me into the house.

"Bad business, that WDC killed on her motorbike?"

"Yes," I said. "Very bad. She was my DC."

He stopped and turned, a look of horror on his face. "I'm sorry, Terry. I didn't know. Saw it on the news last night."

I nodded and followed him into the lounge.

"Sit down, Terry. Do you fancy a coffee? The Mrs is out doing a last bit of holiday shopping."

I wasn't in the mood for coffee. I felt like I was caffeined up to the hilt. "Cheers, Sean, but

I've had about four already, if I have another one, I'll be in the Olympics pissing-team."

He sat in a chair near the fire and I sank into a deep, buttoned Chesterfield. "What do you want to know?"

"I know all the details of the murder, of course, but I've received information that a bloke from Bridgend was responsible. He's got no form at all."

Fair play, Sean didn't even ask the blokes name. He knew I dared not divulge it at this moment in time.

"Okay. Where shall I start?" he thought for a moment. I could nearly see the cogs turning.

"I was working down in Cockett Police Station when I had the call. Porter's van had been found, not far from the village of Shwt, plastered in blood. To be honest, Terry, I had no fucking idea where Shwt was. Never heard of the place. How can you have a place called Shwt? Fucking mental. Anyway, from there on in, it was all hands to the pump. They drafted us in from all over the Force.

"The Senior Investigating Officer was Detective Superintendent John Campbell and his right hand man was DCI Frank Smith. What a fucking pair of twats they were, both from the City, you know, Cardiff, the fucking centre of the universe. To me, they were a pair of useless wankers. I always thought that of them and, by fuck, I was proven right.

"I was on it for nine months, running around like a fucking headless chicken. The top brass never listened to anyone; it was, 'do as I say.' If anyone had an opinion, they just ignored it."

"So, what do you think, Sean, what's your take on the murder?"

"To be honest, Terry, I think they put all their eggs in one basket. Campbell and Smith both believed the murder was committed by a local.

Initially, I thought, 'yes' but as the enquiry progressed, I thought, 'no' there's more to this. Like I say, the two of them didn't really give a fuck what the blokes on the ground thought.

"For the first couple of days, Porter was whiter than white, oh aye, until they found out he was a fucking drug dealer and handler. He became a twat then, and the thinking by the Muppets was it had to be one of his bent associates. When his body was found up by the old colliery in Maesteg, that reinforced it all in the minds of Tweedle-dee and Tweedle-fucking-dum. The killer had to be from the Garw valley.

"That's the way the enquiry went, we were all over the fucking place, Pontycymer, Blaengarw, Maesteg, Llangeinor, Bettws, every-fucking-where. The enquiry just fizzled out; we pulled loads in for questioning, but nothing. Probably the worst murder enquiry I've ever been involved in."

"Did you have any suspects of your own, Sean?"

"One or two, but once they were T.I.E'd, that was the end of them, put on the back burner by that pair of incompetent idiots.

"They were always trying to get one over on each other. If I had been the Detective Chief Super' I'd have got shot of the fucking pair of them and put the divisional fucking CI in charge."

"Were there any sightings at all, Sean, the van, anything at all?"

He shook his head as he thought. "Nothing really, some old girl from Shwt saw a blue van passing through the village, but again, that was dismissed out of hand."

"So what do you reckon, Sean, be honest?"

"Well, I think the whole fucking enquiry was a debacle, I think the two fucking Ronnies thought it was local and that's where it all went wrong. I don't think I can add anymore, Terry. It was a fucking mess, butt. If what you're telling me all works out, Terry, it wouldn't surprise me in the least. I wish you all the best, oh, and by the way, if you detect it, please give me a bell and we'll have a drink on it. Your reputation goes before you. I've heard good things."

I smiled. "I'll keep you to that drink, Sean."

On the way back to the office I was thinking about what Sean had said. Things had progressed since the nineties', senior officers like the two Ronnies were history. But this made me even more determined to detect Porter's murder, if only to rub the undetected murder review team's noses in it.

I knew most of them, and to be honest, if it wasn't for DNA, they wouldn't be able to detect a fucking smell.

THE OLD LADY

John and Caroline arrived back at the office, dead on five o'clock.

"Well, boss, we've been and interviewed the old lady, Lily May Davies, she's in her eighties now but as sharp as a tic. Mrs Davies remembers the murder as if it was yesterday. Bit of excitement for her at the time, I suppose," Caroline said. "She also said the village was awash with Police when the van was found. On the day in question, Mrs Davies was sitting on her chair outside the house, when she saw a blue van drive past at a fast speed towards Bettws hill.

"Mrs Davies didn't get a good look at the driver, only that it was a man wearing a dark coloured baseball hat."

John took over, "Mrs Davies went on to tell us that during the nice weather, she would often sit for hours outside the house and that she knew most of the people who drove or walked through the village..."

"What time of day are we talking about?" I asked.

"Mrs Davies says, it was about four in the afternoon. She remembers because that Ainsley Harriott was on some programme called 'Can't Cook, Won't Cook,' about that time and she was just about to go inside to watch it."

"When was Porter's van discovered, John?"

"Later that evening, boss, just off the road at the bottom of Bettws Hill where all the fly tippers used to dump their crap."

"Then Mrs Davies probably saw the van and the killer?"

"More than likely. Boss."

"Does she remember anything else?"

"No, nothing else, boss. That was about it."

"Well, we still haven't got a lot to go on," I admitted, "but there we are, what can you expect after over twenty years? I think we'll officially arrest Foley for the murder first thing in the morning, that'll give us the whole day to get his prints checked and search his home and the garage."

I gave Mike a shout, and then told him to organise a briefing for seven in the morning with scenes of crime and search teams present.

I managed to go home and spend a couple of hours with Molly and Chris before I hit the sack. I was exhausted. The whiskies with my son help to speed up the onset of slumber.

***

The following morning, I briefed all the officers who would be involved in the arrest and searches.

I outlined the circumstances of the murder to them all.

I pointed out the fact that there was hardly any evidence to implicate Foley in the murder, so it was imperative that the searches were carried out meticulously.

"There are two premises to be searched," I said. "The first is a bed-sit at 200, Nolton Street, in Bridgend. Foley lives there alone since his wife kicked him out of the family home.

"The second premises is located at 42, Meadow Street, a short distance away. This premises houses the garage where Foley services cars. It's also the house hew was living in when the murder took place and Foley's wife still resides there with the children and her fancy man, who, I'm led to believe, owns the house.

"Glyn, I'd like you to do the house and garage because if there's any evidence to be found I think it'll be there."

"No problem, boss. I've had a good look at all the old exhibits, including the tarp used to cover Porter's body, I just hope there may be some lying around in the garage.

Okay then, you all know what teams you're in, let's get cracking. I'll be arresting Foley bang on nine, good hunting."

MICHAEL JEFFREY FOLEY

We arrived at 200, Nolton Street bang on nine. I knocked the door to be greeted by an elderly lady in her fifties, I assumed she was the landlady.

I identified myself to her and asked her to show me to Foley's room. She pointed down the passageway, "He's the first on the left," she touched me on the arm and looked at me with doleful eyes. "Drugs, is it?" she added.

I said nothing. I followed her directions and knocked the door. It was opened by a man who looked about eighty, he was tall, not carrying a lot of weight, unshaven and slightly stooped, It didn't take a genius to see that this man had been ravaged by drugs or drink, or probably both?

"Are you Michael Jeffrey Foley?" I said as I brandished my warrant card.

His expression changed from one of confusion to panic then he nodded. "Yes, that's me."

I didn't want to mess about, what's the point? I had enough to bring him in. I wanted this at an end. "I'm arresting you on suspicion of the murder of Ken Porter in 1995," I said and watched his eyes. He certainly wasn't surprised. Then I cautioned him.

Foley took a large intake of breath, "What happens now?"

I said, "I'll take you to the Bridewell Custody Suite where you'll be detained and later interviewed."

Then, together with Caroline, we loaded Foley into our car, leaving the SOC and search team to get on with their business at his bedsit.

On the way to the Bridewell, Foley remained silent; he just kept looking at the floor, his breathing was erratic. I was worried he was going to have a seizure or heart attack or something.

We arrived at the Bridewell, a custom built facility built to replace the old charge rooms that used to be part of every police station in the division. The idea was to provide a centralised facility to save the cost of keeping the others open. Caroline and I booked Foley in. Mal' OLD was on duty as the custody sergeant and after I'd finished disclosing the facts of the arrest, he authorised Foley's detention.

"Can you sort out the fingerprinting and swabbing of Foley as soon as possible?" I asked Mal.'

"No problem, leave it to me."

I was glad it was Mal' on duty, he knew how I worked and I trusted him to do things right, even if he did have a bit of previous for getting a little hot under the collar.

"Can you get Foley a brief? He hasn't asked for one but he's going to need one."

Foley was a broken man, I wanted to do this by the book and if he was going to cough I wanted his brief there when he did it. "Give me a shout when the brief arrives."

Back in my office, I had a chat with Caroline, "How would you like to be in on the Foley interview with me?"

She grinned. "That would be brilliant, I'm on an aide and I get to sit in on an interview with an alleged murderer? Bloody hell."

I grinned too. I knew how she felt, a similar thing happened to me many years ago, when I was an aide. My DI allowed me in on an Interview with an armed robber, I learned so much that day.

I could see she was genuinely pleased and told her normally I'd normally have a DI or DS with me, but in this case, I'd make an exception.

"What will I have to do, boss?"

"Nothing at all, just listen to how the Interview's structured, you can take a few notes if you like."

To be honest, it suited me to have Caroline in with me. I'm a bit of a control freak when it comes to interviews. I know what I want from the suspect and how to get there. It didn't always pay to have someone else shooting off questions too.

FOLEY INTERVIEW

It was about two hours later when Mal' rang me to say that Foley's brief had arrived.

Rod' Hughes was the duty solicitor, yet again. I knew I had next to nothing in terms of evidence and would now probably have a 'comment' interview for my troubles.

I made my way to the custody suite with Caroline in tow, "Don't be frightened of dealing with high and mighty solicitors, half of them are full of piss and wind," I said. "Have you ever met Mr Rod' Hughes, the solicitor?"

"No boss, but I've heard of him, he's not a very nice bloke by all accounts."

I shook my head. "That's an understatement. He's fucking bent as a corkscrew, got a coke habit and likes young boys. Got a sixteen year old in tow at the moment but I've had the whisper that he's partial to younger lads. Don't care what he does in his spare time but if I get the nod that he's crossed the age line I'll have the bastard."

Caroline looked worried.

"Nothing to worry about," I said.

"It's not that, boss. it's something else. Something I need to speak to you about."

She was going to learn a lot today. I had no idea that I was going to learn something pretty damn important too.

I saw Rod' standing in the doorway of the custody suite. Caroline looked at him and then took me by the arm. She whispered something in my ear and I must admit I began to grin. "Go for it," I said.

I watched as Caroline took Rod' to one side. "Mr Hughes, I've got a disturbing piece of information regarding a flasher that's been causing trouble down in Trecco Bay in Porthcawl..."

"I know where Trecco bay is," Rod' interrupted. "I've got a caravan there."

"Yes, sir, I know. That's why I need to speak to you."

I pretended I couldn't hear all that was being said. In truth, I only heard a few snippets. This was Caroline's baby and I wanted her to bask in the glory of her enquiries.

I heard Rod' say, "Absolute nonsense," and "Can't be," but his face was a picture of concern. He was worried. I let Caroline finish what she had to say and then she nodded to me.

I walked over to them and told Rod' what I had on the Foley case. Surprisingly, Rod' seemed quite amenable, not his usual blustery, arrogant self.

I looked at Mal' and thought perhaps that little episode had changed him? Aye, and pigs will fly. It was Caroline's revelation that had done the trick.

Rod said, "I've conferred with my client and advised him accordingly, this is a very serious allegation."

"Aye, fair enough Rod'" I said. "Let's crack on and get it over with."

We made our way to the Interview room. Caroline got the tapes and prepared everything for what was to come.

A few minutes later, Mal' brought Foley in and sat him on the chair next to Rod.'

I did the usual 'buttering,' told him there was some water if he needed a drink.

Foley thanked me, took a couple of sips from the plastic bottle and then dropped his head. He was looking directly at the table top.

Caroline did the business with the tapes and I went straight into the Interview.

"Michael, you understand that you've been arrested for murder?"

He nodded slowly. "Yes, I understand."

Rod' then stuck his nose in and I thought things were going tits up before we even got started. "Chief Inspector," he said. "I have given my client certain advice, he has gone against it, but I will still be representing him."

I thought, what the fuck is going on here? Rod' has advised no comment, but Foley's ignored the advice?

This time, I had a deep intake of breath.

"Michael, did you know Ken Porter?""

Yes, I did."

"When and how did you meet Porter?"

"I first met him during the miners strike, we were struggling for cash, like all families, and I used to sell stuff to him, things from the house that we didn't need."

"Where was this?"

"Up his second-hand shop in Pontycymer."

"Was this the only relationship you had with Porter?"

"What do you mean, what do you mean by relationship?"

"What other connections did you have with him?"

"Ah, right, he was supplier, I've got a drug habit...but not as bad as it was."

"How long did this relationship go on?"

What happened next took us all by surprise.

"Up until I killed him," he said.

I looked across at Rod,' who remained silent and just raised his eyebrows and shrugged his shoulders.

I was almost dumbstruck. "So, Michael, you're admitting to killing Ken Porter?"

Foley raised his eyes and looked directly into mine. "Yes, I'm sorry. I've lived with this for over twenty years. Look at me; I'm a fucking mess. I've lost everything."

"Will you tell me exactly what, Michael, and why you killed him?

He shrugged. It was as if he really didn't care anymore. "Well, my drug habit got worse after the strike, money was tight and I owed Porter a lot."

"How much did you owe him?"

"I was always in debt to him, but this was about a grand."

"Tell me about the day you killed him, how did that come about?"

"I was in my garage doing a service, it was about midday when he called demanding payment."

"Yes, go on, what happened then?"

"He threatened me, saying, if I didn't get the cash within the next few days he'd have me sorted, together with the Mrs. I didn't mind what the fuck he did to Sian but he threatened my kids' lives too."

"Do you think he would have carried out those threats?"

"No, not him, but he knew enough villains and he'd pay them to do it."

"What happened next?"

"By this time, I was really angry and was laughing at me as he turned away. I just grabbed the nearest thing to hand and hit him on the side of the head."

"With what?"

"A hammer."

What kind of hammer was it Michael?"

I felt it was important to tie him down. It was vital I got all the information. Details are king and would confirm or negate the evidence we already had, what we all ready knew about the injuries.

I could sense that Foley seemed relieved that he'd actually admitted the murder.

"I grabbed my large ball-pein, off my work bench."

"Okay, what happened next?"

He looked at me as if I was mental. "What usually happens when you smack someone over the head with a hammer? He fell to the floor and the blood was pumping out of him. I was going to run but decided to get rid of him instead. I didn't know how, though. It wasn't like I'd had time to plan it. I shut the garage door and just sat on the floor, fucking and blinding, the blood" he shivered, "so much blood."

"What did you do?"

"I had some old tarpaulin, so I cut a big piece off it and wrapped the bastard in it, tied it with rope, opened the garage door and bundled him into the back of his own van."

It seemed to fit what I already knew.

"How many times did you hit Porter?"

He looked mystified. "I don't understand?"

"Well, it's a pretty simple question, how many times did you hit him?"

He nodded and I thought for a moment he was going to clam up. "I thought he was dead," he said, "thought he was dead in the garage, but when I put him in the van I could hear him gurgling."

"So what did you do?"

"So I hit him on the head a few times again," he said, as if it was obvious what he had to do. "Then the gurgling stopped."

"How did you feel about it?"

He shrugged his shoulders. "I knew what I had done was terrible, but I felt relieved, to be honest."

"What happened next?"

"I got in the van, Porter had left the keys in the ignition. I sat there for about five minutes thinking what to do."

"Had you been in the van before?"

"I don't know what you mean?"

He was clearly trying to stay ahead of me. He had thought this through and any question out of the main thread of what he expected was a problem to him. That set alarms ringing.

"Was that the first time you'd been inside the van?"

"Oh, yes. It was the first and only time."

"Porter's body was found in undergrowth near the old St John's colliery in Maesteg. Tell me how it got there?"

"I dumped the bastard up there."

"Why up there, Michael?"

"I just knew the area and thought the further from the garage the better."

"So you're telling me that you drove up to Maesteg and dumped the body?"

"Yes I am and yes I did."

"What time was that, Michael?"

"Mid-afternoon, I think. I lost track of time."

"What did you do after dumping the body?"

"I drove back down the valley, turned down into Shwt and dumped the van at the bottom of the hill."

"Why there?"

He sat back in his chair and sighed as he gazed up at the ceiling and shook his head. "I don't know, I just did it on impulse, to be honest, it was like a fucking nightmare."

"What were you wearing whilst all this was going on?"

Michael seemed to be losing interest. I got the cough but I needed everything tight as a drum. He sat forward and leaned on the table, fingers intertwined beneath his chin. I watched as his fingers kept flexing and closing. "The usual," he said. I wondered what 'the usual' uniform for a murder was. Fair play, he did elaborate. "Jeans, lumber-shirt and steel toe-caps."

"Anything else?"

"What do you mean?"

"Anything on your head?"

"Only my baseball cap."

"What colour?"

"Black, why?"

"A witness believes she saw the van being driven by a man wearing a black baseball cap through Shwt at about four o'clock, would that be you?"

"It must have been. Sounds like it. Look, I didn't mean to kill Porter, but I'm fucking glad I did. He ruined my fucking life, I'm glad it's all over, I'll go to prison. I'll be better off in there. I've got nothing left in my life; no wife and the kids ignore me."

"What did you do with the hammer and ignition keys to the van?"

"I threw the keys into the undergrowth near where I dumped the van. I threw the hammer by the railway line near the bridge going down to Shwt."

"Hang on, Michael," I said, "talk me through that again. You dump the van and throw the keys. I'm interested in the hammer because the Police never recovered one."

He nodded and shrugged his shoulders. "I dumped the van, then walked back up onto the main road, when I got near the bridge, I threw the hammer into the undergrowth by the railway line."

"Will you be able to show me where, Michael?"

"Yes, probably. Been a long time."

"How did you get back home after?".

"I caught the bus, simple as that."

"What about your clothing wasn't there blood on it, weren't you afraid the people on the bus would notice?"

"Nah, I wasn't thinking. Wasn't really any blood on me, not that you'd notice. I burnt it all back at the garage, then cleaned everything up."

I was thinking how the whole thing could have been cleared up at the time if someone had done his or her job properly. "Is there anything else you wish to add Michael?"

"No, that's it. To be honest, I'm glad it's all over. Perhaps I'll sleep now?"

I then terminated the Interview and Foley was returned to the Custody Suite.

I told Mal' about what we had and he further detained Foley. Mal' was grinning and I wondered if he'd heard more of Caroline's conversation with Rod' than I had?

I had a quick chat with Rod' telling him that I'd be taking Foley up to Shwt later in the day for him to point out where he'd thrown the hammer. It was a long shot after all this time but it had to be done.

"I have no doubt I'll be seeing you either later today or early tomorrow, good day, Chief Inspector."

I was itching to know what Rod' had said when Caroline had confronted him earlier. "So," I said. "What's the score with Rod'?"

She shook her head. "Not a lot. Says he has no idea who could have been using his caravan. The Dick of the Dunes might be someone who had hired it at some point and made a spare key?"

"What do you think?" I asked.

"To be honest, boss, I think he's lying. It's obviously not him because he doesn't match the build profile of the flasher but I'm sure he either knows or suspects who it is."

"How do you propose to handle it?"

"Rod' has said he'll try and dig up a list of people who have hired it since he bought it eighteen months ago but he said he bought it second-hand. Could be anybody since the van was sold as new."

I nodded. "It's another piece in the jigsaw. All you can do is check all the names you get and take it a step at a time."

She sighed. "I thought I had the bastard at last."

"You're a step closer. Keep it up. In the meantime, get hold of the search team Inspector and have him meet us up at Shwt in about an hour."

I thought the distraction might help for a while?

"No problem, boss."

By the time I returned to the Office, Glyn Walcott was there with another bit of good news, he had recovered a tarpaulin from the garage, the same type as Porter was wrapped in, he had also taken swabs of practically the whole garage floor for traces of blood.

All the exhibits had been taken by the traffic department to the lab for comparison, again it would all be fast tracked for examination because of the seriousness of the offence and obviously because there was one person in custody. Hopefully, we'd have the result in the morning.

All in all, not a bad result, but the hammer would be the icing on the cake.

FOLEY

I later travelled with Foley up the valley towards Shwt, a small hamlet not too far from Pen-twyn and close to the A4063 from Sarn in the south to Maesteg to the north. I knew the area fairly well, having walked the riverbank of the Llynfi near the railway line a number of times. An old railway bridge still stood, a broken and decrepit memory f the golden age of rail that once brought work and life to the valleys. From what Foley had already told , I was expecting to find the hammer somewhere nearby.

As we approached the railway bridge just off the main road, I could see the search team Inspector with four of his lads. They were fully equipped with all the gear, heavy-duty hedge loppers, strimmers, and rakes and just about everything any self-respecting landscape gardening company would carry. Except, they weren't there to make the place look pretty.

I got Foley out of the vehicle and asked him to show both the inspector and I, where he had thrown the hammer all those years ago.

The railway line was about twenty foot below and the banking was covered in brambles and small bushes. Foley pointed and said, "It's halfway down there, it never went as far as the railway line."

Without any instruction, the search team boys, who had been listening, were over the wire fence with their gear and on the hunt like hounds after a fox.

"Look at them'" the Inspector said, "like kiddies in a playground, they love it, and if it's there they'll find it, boss, I can guarantee that."

Confident, I thought.

The Inspector said, "No need for you to stay, boss, they'll clear this in no time. When we find it I'll give you a bell on your mobile."

I thanked the Inspector, ushered Foley back to the car and began our journey back to the Bridewell.

Now, it was just a matter of waiting for the call. I must admit I wasn't too hopeful.

Anyway, time was getting on. It was getting dark and Caroline must have plied me with about ten cups of coffee. We chatted about the Dick of the Dunes and I have to say I was impressed with her efforts. Her hands had been tied and there wasn't an awful lot she could do but she had done everything that I would have done. Couldn't ask for more.

I had just unzipped my pants to relieve myself of some of that coffee when my mobile rang, I nearly dropped the bloody thing down the urinal. It was the search Inspector, "It's not good news, my boys have cleared a massive area around where Foley said he threw the hammer, but they can't find it."

That's all I needed at this stage. What made it worse was the fact that I nearly lost my mobile down the pisser for shit news. All I had now was the cough and I now believed Foley was taking the piss about the hammer.

I can see Rod,' now making representations about duress, the slimy bastard.

"Thanks," I said. Tell your lads I'm grateful for their effort. You can bring your kids in from the playground now," I added. He laughed and apologised again.

"Shit happens!"

I returned to the custody suite and asked Mal' to get Rod' back out because I wanted to interview Foley again to clear up the hammer business.

Half an hour later, we were all back in the interview room, myself, Caroline, Rod' and Foley.

Again, Caroline did the business with the tapes and I began to speak to Foley. "Michael, the search team can't find any trace of the hammer in the area you showed us, what have you got to say about that?"

I saw Foley's left eye begin to twitch. That was a new one on me. "That's where I threw it," he said. "Perhaps someone picked it up?"

Foley then sat back in his chair and began swinging gently on the back legs. His demeanour had changed in an instance. He now appeared far more confident and I wondered if he finally realised what he'd admitted?

I was beginning to feel uneasy about all this. "Picked it up," I said, "you saw the under growth, I hope you're not lying about this, Michael?"

Then it happened. "No Comment," he said.

"What?" I growled. "No comment, what's going on, Michael?"

Rod' chipped in, "On my instructions, Chief Inspector."

I tried to hide my frustration but I'm sure they noticed me slump in my chair. "Is there any point in putting further questions to your client, Mr Hughes?"

He replied, "I don't think so, Chief Inspector."

Rod's back on form. I thought, fuck him, I'll charge Foley anyway. I still had his confession and the tarpaulin, that would be enough for any Jury.

"Is there anything you would like to add, Michael, because after this interview, I will be formally charging you with the murder of Ken Porter.

"No Comment."

I terminated the interview and looked across the table at Rod' as he popped the cap back on his fancy Parker and dropped his notebook into his expensive looking briefcase. The bastard was smiling. I felt like leaning over the table, taking the pen from his pocket and shoving it up his nose, the twat.

Instead, I returned Foley to the custody suite, informed Mal' that I'd now charge Foley with murder.

"No problem, boss?

Mal' still had that stupid vacant grin he always had when he knew something I didn't. "We'll formulate the charge and I'll give you a ring when ready," he said.

Mal' then tilted his head and looked towards a quiet corner. I presumed he wanted me to follow him. I decided to play his game. He leaned in to me and began to whisper in my ear, "By the way, I had them fast-track Foley's fingerprints to compare with any left in the van. Guess what?"

L pulled my best 'don't fuck me about' face. "I don't know," I said. "Fucking tell me."

Mal' looked affronted. "Ooowww, stroppy fucker, are we?"

I had to laugh. We'd known each other too long to stand on ceremony.

"There's a full palm print that matches Foley."

I grabbed Mal's ears and pulled him to me and kissed him on the forehead. "I love you, you miserable old fucker. If I was a woman I'd have your babies."

"If you were a woman I wouldn't be seen dead with you, not with that goatee."

I turned to Rod and broke the good news. I asked if he would like to be present when I charged Foley, but the bastard had a 'prior engagement.'

He walked out of the Bridewell whilst I tried to burn a big hole in his back with my Vulcan death glance. Didn't work. I dearly wanted to bang the fat bastard up; perhaps I would put him on my hit list if Caroline didn't.

Half an hour later, I formally charged Foley with the murder of Ken Porter, when cautioned he replied, "Thank God it's all over, I couldn't live with that any longer. I'm sorry."

I thought to myself, would you have said that if Rod' had been present? I doubted it.

After charging Foley, he was further detained, pending court, and then he'd be remanded to Cardiff Prison to await his appearance at the Crown Court.

I must admit, initially I did feel a bit sorry for Foley; he'd been a victim of circumstances all those years ago. First the strike, then his Mrs on the game, the drink, the drugs, losing his kids, he had no chance. However, the second interview showed a different side to him.

Very, very, sad.

I turned to Caroline, "Have you learnt anything from all this today?"

She smiled, "Yes, boss. It's made me even more determined to become a detective."

"Do me a favour?" I said.

"What's that, boss?"

"Catch that Dick of the Dunes first."

"Don't worry, boss. I intend to."

THE FUNERAL

I stood with Molly and my son in the entrance to Abercrave Church as the hearse, led by two police motorcycle outriders, crawled up the final stretch of driveway. The weather seemed to reflect the mood of all those present. A grey sky spat a drizzle down onto the gathered crowd. I looked across the sea of heads, the line of uniformed officers standing to attention – the guard of honour – her motorcycle helmet rested in the centre of the Police flag draped over the coffin as it was gently lifted from the hears and carried into the crumbling building. The church had seen much better days. It had become the victim of erosion over decades and looked sad and forlorn.

We packed into the church, leaving twice as many friends and colleagues outside in the rain.

I sat near the back and listened to the vicar read from a prepared eulogy about a young woman I thought I knew. It was only when I listened to the truncated anecdotes about Jane that I realised I didn't really know her at all. I knew she was a single mother of a little boy called Jack. I knew she was twenty-eight and lived in Bridgend. I knew her husband had served in the Police but had left to start his own business, something to do with Graphic Design or advertising?

I didn't know that she was one of two sisters. Jane had grown up nearby in the village of Caehopkin. I didn't know that she had been accepted to study Law at Oxford University, and I didn't know she had turned it down to join the job. She even worked as a barmaid on weekends before she became a copper. I shook my head as more and more of her backstory was revealed and I felt ashamed of myself. I should have known.

Molly leaned into me and hooked her arm in mine.

I then got the call to the front and strolled down to the altar to deliver my prepared speech. I pulled the sheet from my pocket then folded it again. A prepared eulogy wasn't going to be appropriate. I had to offer more than that.

I stood and took a deep breath.

"We shouldn't be here today. We shouldn't be celebrating the life of Jane. We shouldn't be saying goodbye to a daughter, a mother, a friend. There are many of us here who have had good lives, we've taken opportunities, lived our lives and had the time to moan those older than us when their time came to leave us.

"Jane should be standing here, reading a eulogy for me or…more likely, for Mal' Old…"

The congregation laughed. I knew Mal' was there somewhere but he was lost in the sea of black-clad and uniformed bodies.

"It's at times like this that we remember that life is cruel. It's often punctuated by happiness and love, but ultimately it's cruel. Jane had so much to live for. She was vibrant, she was enthusiastic and forever keen to do the job to the best of her ability, and that ability seemed to have no limits. I had only worked with her a few short months but in that time I'd like to think we formed a bond, a bond that only people in our position can ever truly understand. Jane dealt with whatever was thrown at her with dignity and total professionalism. She handled most things with a smile and if a job needed doing it would be Jane's hand that would shoot up, especially if riding a motorbike was anyway involved," there were more chuckles.

"It's at times like this that we realise our family is the most important thing in life. Nothing else really matters. We try to make an impact whilst we're here, to make the world just a little bit better than it would have been had we not been born. Whether we achieve that or not makes no difference. What matters is that we try. Jane tried and Jane did make a difference. She made a difference to her parents; she made a difference to her sister, her son and a major difference to the Squad. She made a difference to me.

"We are here for a very short time. All I want to do now is throw in my badge and go home and spend the rest of my days with my wife and children. It's so tempting."

I looked for Molly and could see her wiping tears from her eyes.

"But people like Jane make sacrifices that are often scorned by others, people who hide behind their curtains because they are too scared to stand up for themselves. It's part of the job. We signed up to be the person who steps between that curtain dweller and the thug that wants to steal those curtains.

"Most of you in this room should leave here knowing that it doesn't matter what others think of you. It's your family, friends and colleagues that stand by you, they are the ones that understand and they are the only ones that really matter.

"Jane was the epitome of the officer we should all strive to be. I can't help but wonder what she would have achieved had she lived just a little bit longer?"

I turned towards the coffin, "God bless you, Jane," I said and walked back to my family.

The wake was a surprisingly upbeat function. Held in the New Swan pub in nearby Ystalyfera, the bar she worked in during her youth. The jukebox softly played a medley of Jane's favourite music and I stood quietly at the bar and listened to the tales of Jane from those who knew her far better than me.

I met her mother and father and felt their pain. It seemed such a pointless loss. I toasted their daughter, said my farewells and Chris drove us home.

***

Molly and I stood in the departures lounge of Heathrow Airport. I'd taken a couple of days off to spend at least some time with my wife and son before he travelled back to Hong Kong.

I talked about all the things I promised to do with Chris next time he was home and must have apologised a dozen times for not being with him this time around. I think he understood.

I held Molly tight as we watched his plane take off, bank onto its course and disappear through the clouds.

"It'll be different next time. Molly. I swear."

She hugged me and looked up into my eyes. She knew I meant it but she'd lived with a copper long enough to know that things rarely ever worked out as planned.

She sighed. "Whilst there's kids dying from stupid shit and people making it happen, you'll always be there, Terry..."

I shook my head. "Not next time, Molly."

She turned my head towards her and she kissed me tenderly. "I love you for who you are, You'll never change and I don't want you to. You make a difference, like you said in the funeral. As long as you're out there I'll always feel safe."

Terry McGuire will be back...

Read on for an extract of the forthcoming Terry McGuire thriller: ANGEL OF DEATH

ANGEL OF DEATH

Terry McGuire Thriller Book 4

THE OLD WOMAN OF THE GOWER

The old woman emptied the contents of the plastic bucket into the sink and squeezed the dirty water from the cloth before dropping it into the bucket and storing it in a cupboard beneath the kitchen window.

She gazed through the newly cleaned pane at the sea sparkling in the beams of sunlight breaking through the heavy grey clouds.

Leaning on the chipped and discoloured Belfast sink, she sighed, a release of a pervasive apprehension that had possessed her soul for far too long, the exorcism of phantoms of the past, the evil sprites of spiteful memories.

The view was spectacular, something that had attracted her to the place over forty years ago. It never ceased to raise her spirits, however down she felt.

The kitchen was small, dark and Spartan, a time capsule, untouched since it was built nearly a century ago. There had been no concessions to modernity over the years. No hot running water, no central heating, no electricity, no gas and certainly no television or phone line, but it was as she liked it. She had never wanted anything other than a retreat, a place to sit and contemplate, to make sense of her memories and to write in safety.

The old lady took a dry cloth from a drawer and began wiping down surfaces she thought her visitor had touched. No one could know who had paid her a visit. Her whole life had been lived through a collection of secrets and even now she couldn't break the habit.

Satisfied, she stepped slowly to the threadbare armchair pulled close to the dying embers of the wood fire and lowered herself into the hard cushion that had once been soft, now compressed over years of use. Her bones ached and her muscles were stiff. Age really didn't come alone.

She took a small album of photos from the table alongside her chair and flipped open the cover. Inside were images of another world from many years before, a life she had devoted to others and to her God, a life she had been forced to escape, a personal decision that had been life changing, that had profoundly affected so many people, and the focus of a deep regret for the pain she had caused.

She wiped a tear from her eye and snapped the album shut. The memories were too painful. There had been a time, long, long ago, when the tears would not stop, but time diminishes pain even if it doesn't heal it completely.

The album was swapped for the hand written notes she kept bound within an old desk diary dated 1970. Each page had been filled with notes, not with the usual entries one would expect within a diary. These notes were far more personal and far more explosive. She knew that they would one day be read by someone and now was the time, just not whilst she was still alive. She knew the cancer would take her soon and that she would have to face the eternal consequences of her actions, but until that moment arrived she still had more to write.

The old woman picked up her pen and began to add to her notes.

THE PARK

He sat on the park bench, close to the old man, and watched a small boy launch large chunks of bread at the ducks. He chuckled as a Warburton's Exocet struck a Mallard across the beak and ricocheted into the eager path of a young swan.

"Brought up on a council estate I was. An only child I was. My father was an HGV driver, so he wasn't home much," he told the old man who sat wrapped up in a heavy overcoat beneath what the locals called a 'Dai cap.' The old man said nothing. His rheumy eyes watered in the chill breeze, a pair of tears raced down his cheeks to the warm wool scarf beneath his chin.

"He wasn't a very nice man, often beat me and mam for no reason.

"Mam was a drunk but I loved her. I'd come home from school and she'd be lying in a pool of sick. I had to clean her and put her to bed.

"I was always being bullied by bigger boys in school. Didn't have any friends, in fact I hated school, I hated everybody. My father didn't give a toss about my mam, always giving her the odd clip, she was scared to death of him," he shifted his position on the cold wooden slats of the bench that were aching his glutes. "I think being drunk was her way of dulling the pain. He was hardly ever home, he loved the women, he was a bastard.

"I basically had to fend for myself. Most of the time, I would be alone in my room staring at the four walls."

The old man shifted uncomfortably too and the younger man continued his monologue as he checked the old man was okay. "As I got older and wiser, I tried to get my mam some help, but it was no good, the drink had finished her. I loved my mam.

"One day, when I was about fourteen, I came home from school and my mother was in the kitchen making chips in a saucepan, you know, like we used to do before we had one of those electric fryers," he began to smile at the memory. "My father came in, he was in a temper, as normal, for no reason. He slapped my mother across the face, and she went flying across the room," the smile was replaced by a frown. "He went to hit her again, her nose was bleeding, and he was standing over her, ready to lay into her. I got in between them and pulled his arm back and he smacked me across the head and sent me flying as well.

"He grabbed my mother by the hair and started dragging her across the kitchen floor."

A fight broke out between some of the birds, jostling to get the next Warburton's sample from the sadistic toddler. The sound of frantic ducks was momentarily deafening and he thought it was a good representation of the fight he was recalling at home many years before. "Jesus, look at them buggers going for it," the younger man said. He waited for the noise to abate in a flurry of dislodged feathers before continuing.

"It was then that I picked up the saucepan full of chip fat and threw it all over the bastard's head and face," he grinned again, "he fell on the floor screaming, I laughed at the bastard, seeing him in pain, and I couldn't be bothered even to help him, in fact I felt like stabbing him, too.

"I picked mam up and walked her into the lounge, all she wanted was a drink.

"My father was still screaming in the kitchen, I went back to see him, he was rolling on the floor, holding his face. He got to his feet and I thought, this is the last time you'll lay your hands on me or my mam, and I kicked him straight between the legs and he went down like a sack of shit.

"I leaned over him saying, 'you're lucky I haven't fucking killed you.'

The younger man sat upright and inflated his chest. "Do you know something? I felt great, and from that day on he never laid a hand on us, every time I saw the scars on his face and neck I felt proud.

Since then, nobody and I mean nobody fucks about with me."

He sat quietly for a moment then turned to the old man. "I might as well talk to the fucking ducks, you deaf, old bastard."

END

If you enjoyed the Terry McGuire thrillers please take a few minutes to write a review. All good reviews help us in our drive to raise money for Marie Curie Cancer Trust.

Thank you.

End of Preview

14784354R00165

Printed in Poland
by Amazon Fulfillment
Poland Sp. z o.o., Wrocław